BARBARA CARTLAND'S LIBRARY OF LOVE

No one writes romantic fiction like Barbara Cartland.

Miss Cartland was originally inspired by the best of the romantic novelists she read as a girl—Elinor Glyn, Ethel M. Dell, Ian Hay and E. M. Hull. Convinced that her own wide audience would also delight in her favorite authors, Barbara Cartland has taken their classic tales of romance and specially adapted them for today's readers.

BARBARA CARTLAND'S LIBRARY OF LOVE

1. *The Sheik* E. M. Hull
2. *His Hour* Elinor Glyn
3. *The Knave of Diamonds* Ethel M. Dell
4. *A Safety Match* Ian Hay
5. *The Hundredth Chance* Ethel M. Dell
6. *The Reason Why* Elinor Glyn
7. *The Way of an Eagle* Ethel M. Dell
8. *The Vicissitudes of Evangeline* Elinor Glyn
9. *The Bars of Iron* Ethel M. Dell
10. *Man and Maid* Elinor Glyn
11. *The Sons of the Sheik* E. M. Hull
12. *Six Days* Elinor Glyn
13. *Rainbow in the Spray* Pamela Wynne
14. *The Great Moment* Elinor Glyn
15. *Greatheart* Ethel M. Dell
16. *The Broad Highway* Jeffrey Farnol
17. *The Sequence* Elinor Glyn
18. *Charles Rex* Ethel M. Dell
19. *Ashes of Desire* Pamela Wynne
20. *The Price of Things* Elinor Glyn
21. *Tetherstones* Ethel M. Dell
22. *The Amateur Gentleman* Jeffrey Farnol
23. *His Official Fiancée* Berta Ruck
24. *The Lion Tamer* E. M. Hull
25. *It* Elinor Glyn

Barbara Cartland's Library of Love

THE SONS
OF THE SHEIK
BY E.M. HULL
CONDENSED BY
BARBARA CARTLAND

DUCKWORTH

Casebound edition first published 1980 by
Gerald Duckworth & Co Ltd
The Old Piano Factory
43 Gloucester Crescent
London NW1

Copyright 1925 by Edith M. Hull
Copyright renewed 1952 by Cecil Winstanley Hull
This edition copyright © 1977 by
Barbara Cartland

All rights reserved. No part of this
publication may be reproduced, stored in a
retrieval system, or transmitted, in any
form or by any means, electronic, mechanical,
photocopying, recording or otherwise, without
the prior permission of the publisher.

ISBN 0 7156 1472 X

Printed in Great Britain by
Billing & Sons Limited
Guildford, London and Worcester

Introduction
By
Barbara Cartland

Everyone who loved *The Sheik* and longed to know what happened afterwards to Diana and her desert lover will enjoy this book. The Sheik's sons are as strong, self-willed, and compelling as he was. They are also fated to fight for love and be conquered by the force and power of it.

"Yasmin—my love—Yasmin," will ring in your ears long after you have finished this book.

Chapter One

The dawn wind was blowing keenly across the desert.

Shapeless in heavy close-drawn cloaks, their backs bent to the blast, three horsemen rode slowly through the gloom, pursuing a cautious way over broken rocky ground.

It was no road to travel in the darkness.

But despite the nervousness of the horses, whose trembling limbs and snorting breaths showed their uneasiness, despite the occasional smothered ejaculations of two of the party, the little troop went steadily on.

The leader, muffled in a black burnous which, enveloping him, hung down on either side of the saddle and seemed to merge imperceptibly into the glossy blackness of his horse, was almost invisible in the obscurity.

Riding a few paces behind him, his companions, white-clad, appeared like two attendant spectres.

Little by little the blackness of night gave way to the birth of a new day, and finally the first outlying spur of the hills was reached, the horses checking suddenly in a great slithering rush that brought them to the very foot of a steep rock that rose sheer and jagged above their heads.

The leader dismounted and, turning his horse over to one of his men, stood for a few minutes looking fixedly in the direction from which he had come.

Seemingly about twenty years of age, tall and and slenderly built, though with wide shoulders that gave promise of further development, he carried himself arrogantly.

His handsome face, lean, and bronzed with the sun, was clean-shaven, displaying a firm, obstinate chin and a straight, somewhat cruel mouth.

Thick black brows, drawn together in a heavy scowl, shaded a pair of dark blue eyes that at the moment were sombre with thought.

Shrugging slightly, as if dismissing an unpleasant recollection, he flung back his heavy burnous and, swinging on his heel, went to join his men, who, standing close together and conversing in undertones, had been watching him intently.

Of these, one was as tall and slender as his leader, and the other was short and more heavily built, but an unmistakable similarity of features and expression proclaimed them brothers.

They drew apart at his coming, and the shorter of the two, who seemed the elder, offered him some dates from a bag he had taken from the saddle.

Refusing them, the young man dropped down onto the sand, and, settling himself comfortably with his back against a rock, took a gold case from the pocket of his silk *gandoura* and lit a cigarette.

For nearly half an hour he remained smoking, preserving a silence his followers were careful not to break. But their eyes rarely left his face, and they both were obviously uneasy.

At last the young Chief rose to his feet and signalled for his horse. But the laughing jest that accompanied his order died on his lips as he saw the men return leading their own horses also.

He made a curt gesture of dismissal.

"No need for them. I go alone," he said peremptorily, catching the bridle of his plunging mount and manoeuvring to get his foot into the stirrup the elder man held for him.

"You shall wait for me here, Ramadan—it was understood. You also, S'rir," he added sharply over his shoulder to the younger brother, who was already halfway into the saddle.

There followed a storm of protest, a duet of heated expostulations which ranged from abject entreaties to expressions of open rebellion.

But entreaties and arguments alike failed to alter the Chief's decision.

Mounted now, and restraining with difficulty his impatient horse, he stared down at his excited, gesticulating followers with visible annoyance that augmented rapidly until, quite suddenly, he lost his temper.

"Be silent!" he stormed. "Do I give orders, or do you? Didn't you hear? Must I speak again? I go alone."

Ramadan's hand clenched on the stirrup he still held.

"We would go also," he persisted.

"And why?"

The man's eyes wavered, but he held his ground obstinately.

"It is not safe," he muttered reluctantly, as if the words were forced from him.

For a moment the Chief's eyes flashed ominously. Then, like the passing of a summer storm, his anger evaporated in a peal of boyish laughter.

"Safe—O timid maid!" he mocked. "Since when have you thought of safety, Ramadan?"

"Your safety, Lord, not mine," retorted Ramadan hotly.

"Mine or yours, it's all alike, and all foolishness. No, Ramadan, no more. I go alone. Wait till I return."

"And if you do not return?"

The Chief's sharp, shovel-shaped stirrup touched his horse's flank, making him rear almost perpendicularly and forcing the Arab to quit his hold.

"If I do not return," he cried with a reckless laugh, "then look for me in Heaven or Hell, for you will certainly penetrate to both in search of me."

With a wave of the hand he was gone, in a swirl of dust and sand.

Together the two brothers watched him until a jutting spur of rock hid him from sight. Then they faced each other, the elder cursing deeply, the younger smiling enigmatically.

"If harm comes to him—what of my Lord?" burst out Ramadan suddenly.

S'rir's smile became a grin in which there was no mirth, and he made an expressive gesture that was very significant.

"Say rather—what of us?" he returned meaningly.

But the next minute he shrugged, with real or assumed indifference, his eyes sweeping upwards to the sun.

"Three hours, he told us last night," he remarked calmly. "So be it. For three hours we will wait, and if in three hours he doesn't return, then brother, we are likely to see either heaven or hell. Meanwhile, I sleep."

And with a short laugh he pulled the hood of his burnous over his head and curled up on the sand.

But, far beyond the spur of rock that hid him from his followers' anxious gaze, the rider on the big black horse was speeding across the desert with no hint of trouble on his handsome face.

Forgetful of his men's insistence, of his own short outburst of temper, conscious only of his youth, his strength, and of the pleasure awaiting him, he rode at breakneck pace towards a second spur of rock that, like the one behind him, jutted out into the sand a mile or two away.

Somewhere amongst the labyrinthine hills she waited for him, the slim shy maiden of his fancy. But here he was in a strange country, and, himself a stranger, it behoved him to go warily.

For who knew what other ears than hers were listening for his coming?

Pulling his horse to a walk, he rounded the knife-edged spur, and keeping close in to the farther side, rode slowly parallel with it until he reached the bare rock face that formed the southern boundary of the hills.

Rising sheer, and seemingly inaccessible, the only inlet was a narrow defile cut by the passage of some ancient river long since dried up.

Crossing the little depression, after he had dismounted, with long springy strides the young man started to climb the opposite hillside. It was bad going; the rocks were slippery and the loose ground gave continually beneath his feet.

But, active as a cat and in perfect physical condition, he climbed steadily, undeterred by his voluminous burnous and high riding-boots.

Following the almost obliterated traces of an

old track that zig-zagged up the steep slope, he reached at last the summit of the hill, where there was a little plateau, and stood for a moment looking searchingly about him.

He had expected to find her on the plateau, but the little tableland was devoid of life.

Again he jerked his head impatiently, his quick temper flaming. How much farther did she imagine he would go in response to the ambiguous message that had reached him?

He had ridden hot-foot during the night—was he to spend all day hunting for a maid he had stooped to notice?

Scowling fiercely, he hesitated, torn between desire that bade him go forward and a sense of pride that urged him to retrace his steps.

Then he smiled a trifle grimly. To punish her was to punish himself, and having come so far he was in no mind to return without seeing her.

Throwing back his burnous to free his arms, he strode on down the hill, his hand on the butt of the revolver hidden in his waistcloth.

Once free of the plateau, the trail was a blind one, for the huge boulders hemming him in on every side made only a few yards of the way visible.

His senses keenly on the alert, he rounded each one swiftly and noiselessly, plunging farther and farther down the hillside until a sudden sound brought him to an abrupt halt; he listened intently.

A thin little reedy sound it was, echoing somewhere from among the rocks to the right of where he stood.

He turned aside and followed it. In and out of the boulders he went, treading softly, until he came to a small semi-circular recess set between two high walls of rock.

Opposite him a great rent in the cliff face gave an open view of the desert as though from the broken window of a ruined building.

And close by this natural peephole sat a slender slip of a girl who seemed barely to have left childhood behind her.

Dressed in a black kilted skirt and short brocaded jacket, a bright sash folded about her waist, a velvet sequinned cap stuck jauntily on the side of her little head, she was swaying slowly to and fro, holding a *guesbo* to her lips.

Unaware as yet of his presence, her whole attention was fixed on a basket set on the ground before her, from the wide-open mouth of which protruded the flat narrow head and sinuous length of a big black snake.

Looping and coiling, making slow feints and passes with its head, the creature was responding, fascinated, to the halting rhythm of the weird, elusive melody its mistress was drawing from the little Arab flute.

For perhaps a minute the young man stood watching the lazy evolutions of the reptile, and the pliant figure of the youthful musician, then he said:

"*Salamalik.*"

His deep-voiced greeting was like the breaking of a spell.

With an angry hiss the snake slipped swiftly over the side of the basket and vanished amongst the rocks, while the girl leaped to her feet with a tinkle of silver anklets and faced him, wide-eyed and panting.

Poised like a wild creature meditating flight,

she seemed both half-glad and half-fearful of his coming.

As he went to her she turned away with a little petulant gesture.

"You are late," she murmured reproachfully.

"Yet, since I am here, what does it matter?" he answered lightly.

But her welcome was not the one he had expected, and his passionate temper quickened.

"Why are you here?" he demanded with abrupt masterfulness. "I told you to meet me on the plateau at dawn."

"It is safer here," she whispered, with a shiver.

But already her eyes were turning to him wistfully.

And scowling down at her in the full flush of his youthful arrogance, he caught her furtive glance of mingled awe and appeal, and his face softened while a strange new feeling ran through him that was like an actual stab of pain.

His slim brown hands shot out to grip her shoulders. It was the first time that he had ever touched her, and his heart beat furiously as his fingers slowly tightened.

"Yasmin—Yasmin!" he cried with a gasp, and swept her into his arms.

Young as he was, he had played with love before, many times. This morning he had thought to play with it again, but fate had tripped him up.

For now the close contact of her was awakening him to a knowledge of something deeper and stronger than he had ever before known.

His burning gaze devouring her, he drew her closer and still closer, but the goal that had driven him headlong through the night seemed all at once impossible.

He did not understand himself, did not attempt to fathom the impulse that stayed him. He realised only the sudden sense of self-disgust that had come to him, the instinct to spare when he had never spared before.

And as he wrestled with himself he could feel her shuddering against him, her supple little body rigid and unbending in his embrace, could see the terror that lay in her big, beseeching eyes.

With a tremendous effort he flung desire from him.

"What do you fear, little trembling one? Is my love so evil that I should harm you? See, is it so very dreadful a thing—my kiss?"

Stooping his tall head suddenly, he laid his lips full on her upturned scarlet mouth.

It was an un-Arab form of caress, but he was not prepared for the sharp cry that burst from her, nor for the almost hysterical flood of tears that followed.

"Soul of my soul, how have I hurt you?" he cried.

But for a time she could not answer. Yielding to his arms at last, she clung to him, her face buried in his burnous, weeping as if her heart would break.

Mystified by something beyond his understanding, he waited silently for her explanation.

She lifted her head at last, looking at him timidly.

"Forgive me, Lord," she whispered with a long sobbing breath; "you have not hurt me. It was only that long ago... they kissed me like that... when I was a child... and happy."

He stared at her with a puzzled frown.

"They?... Who?"

But she shook her head as if unwilling or unable to enlighten him.

"I have forgotten," she replied evasively, her eyes wavering under his.

Hand in hand they climbed up to the natural peephole and sat down on a broad shelf of rock overlooking the desert.

For a long time he did not speak. His chin cupped in the palm of his hand, his elbow on his knee, he studied her intently, as though he were seeing her for the first time.

It was a very beautiful little face he looked on, a face strangely sensitive and refined.

A wealth of night-black hair shaded features that were regular and well-cut: a short, delicately shaped nose, small mouth, and shy, expressive brown eyes that owed nothing to the kohl that darkened their thick curling lashes.

And from her face his gaze wandered appraisingly over the slim length of her till at last she moved uneasily under his passionate stare, her cheeks flushing hotly.

One small brown hand stole out to him.

"Do I please you?"

With a half-mocking, half-tender smile, he drew her down till her head rested against his breast.

"You are not so ill," he conceded teasingly.

But the light that shone in his dark eyes satisfied her, and for a while she lay still, playing with the golden tassel of his burnous while she listened with a faint smile to his highly imaginative account of the perils of his midnight ride.

But her attention was only perfunctory, and her thoughts obviously were wandering, for at last she broke in on his narrative, looking up at him with shy intentness.

"Who are you, Lord? You have never told me. I do not even know your name."

His lips curved in a half-smile.

"I am he who loves you. Is it not enough, O daughter of curiosity?"

"Tell me your name," she persisted, undeterred by the evasive answer.

For a few moments he did not speak. His black brows drawn together in a heavy scowl, his mouth set obstinately, he stared down at her almost fiercely, as if seeking to probe for what lay hidden behind her insistence.

Then with a light laugh he pushed her away and lit a cigarette, still watching her from behind the wreathing smoke.

"I am called—Ahmed," he said at length.

She started, and a faint look of fear shadowed her face.

"Ahmed," she repeated slowly. "I have heard of a great Lord beyond the mountains in the South, the ruler of the tribe of Ben Hassan, who bears that name. Are you akin to him?"

Surprised, he shot her a searching glance that he masked behind indolent half-closed eyes, and then smiled lazily.

"Who knows?" he answered carelessly. "Why do you ask? What have you heard of Ahmed ben Hassan?"

He uttered the question with seeming indifference, stooping forward to flick a grey curl of cigarette ash in the path of a hurrying scavenger beetle.

A shudder went through her and she crept closer, peeping nervously over her shoulder as though she dreaded some unseen listener.

"That he is a demon," she whispered fearfully, her wide eyes full of awe. "No true Arab born of woman but an afreet whom all fear for his strength and power, which is above that of mortal man; one who rules his tribe by sorcery and enchantment, who rides swifter than the tempest, and whose eye blasts like the fiery bolt from Heaven.

"And he cannot die, for many have sought to kill him, and failed. That I have heard, and more I dare not tell you, in case..."

She broke off suddenly and drew back, trembling with superstitious terror, striving to read his inscrutable face.

"Are you sure that you are not akin to him?"

With a little laugh he caught and held her fast.

"And if I were, would you love me less?"

For a fraction of a minute she hesitated, shivering in his grasp.

Then a great sob burst from her.

"No...no!" she cried, and clung to him. "Demon or man, I love you...and I never loved before!"

Her little cap had fallen off, and the scent of her dark hair was like a subtle intoxicant as he bent over her, triumphant, and exulting in her beauty.

"Yasmin, my love, my flower of delight, was ever a maid so fair!"

Speech had almost drifted into silence, and, drawn a little apart, they sat gazing into each other's eyes, lost in the wonder of their happiness.

So still did they sit that the chattering, eager birds ignored their presence, and a sand-grey lizard ran out on a rock nearby to watch them, unafraid.

The warming rays of the sun brought no remembrance of the passing time; unnoticed, the long moments crept slowly by.

He had forgotten his men, forgotten the danger of these robber-haunted hills, forgotten everything but the girl who knelt at his feet, with her slim hands clasped in her lap.

Absorbed, his ears heard nothing but the music of her low soft tones, and his ardent eyes saw only the marvel of her delicate loveliness.

And in the end it was she, facing what was hidden from him, who saw; she who uttered the choking little cry that sent him stumbling to his feet as a bullet went *spat!* against the rock where a second before his head had rested.

Wrenching the revolver from his waistband, he thrust her behind him and wheeled to confront his assailant.

But, as he turned, a burning flame leaped across his forehead and he reeled, his own shot going wide.

He had a momentary glimpse of three tall white-clad figures; then, blinded with the blood that poured down his face, he staggered a step forward and pitched headlong from the shelf of the rock.

It was a ten-foot drop, and, landing, his right shoulder struck the edge of a sharp, unyielding boulder. Broken or dislocated he knew it was, and he set his teeth as he tried to roll over, his left hand groping for the weapon that had fallen under him.

Giddy with the shock and sick with pain, he had risen to his knees when a crashing blow on the head sent him sprawling on his face again.

With a roaring as of the sea in his ears, he seemed to feel himself falling swiftly down, down into abysmal blackness.

* * *

Through waves of sickening nausea he struggled back to life, conscious only at first of an agonising pain in his head, then of a raging thirst that was torment.

A half-understood sense of danger made him attempt to move, but at the first effort he collapsed, his head swimming, his body drenched in perspiration.

For a while he lay still, with closed eyes, striving to regain command of himself, to pierce the thick fog that seemed to have settled over his brain.

He had no recollection of what had happened; even his past life was a blank, from which only one thing emerged clearly and distinctly.

He remembered his name.

He was Ahmed ben Hassan, and someone had said that his Father was a demon. But that was a stupid jest. For if it were so, how could "the little Mother," who, he knew for a fact, was an angel, ever have married him?

And yet, who was "the little Mother"? And who, indeed, was Ahmed ben Hassan?

To think was agony, but painfully he laboured with the perplexing questions his dazed brain refused to answer, until thought became at last impossible, and a rush of helpless anger went through him and left him exhausted and muttering incoherently.

Then came fear, a paralysing feeling of pure terror; terror of himself, terror of the mental darkness that enveloped him. With a strangled cry he relapsed into unconsciousness.

An hour or two later he woke again, in full possession of his senses.

A deep groan burst from him, and for a few moments he wrestled desperately, with death in his heart, in a futile attempt to loosen the cords that bound him.

But the work had been done too thoroughly, and, realising that he was expending uselessly what strength remained to him, he soon gave up the struggle and lay still, his face working convulsively.

It was not of himself that he was thinking.

He could await his own fate with the stoical indifference that was partly an inherited trait, partly the result of lifelong training. Whether he lived or died was, for the moment, of no consequence insofar as it affected himself.

It was the girl who filled his mind. It was for her that he was agonising. Into what peril had his thoughtless folly brought her? In what desperate strait might she be even at this moment, as he lay trussed like a beast, and powerless to help her!

Yasmin—Yasmin! His slender maiden of delight!

Was some other hand, ruder and rougher than his, to cull and bruise the tender flower he had thought to cherish in the garden of his love?

It was for his sake that she had braved the terrors of those ill-famed hills. It was his own proud arrogance that had prompted him to ride alone to meet her, disdaining the escort whose vigilance would have prevented the catastrophe that had come so suddenly and tragically upon them.

She had trusted him, and as man and lover he had failed her utterly.

Shame and remorse overwhelmed him, and a deadly fear, which set him straining frantically at his bonds again.

"Yasmin," he whispered, with shaking lips, "my little love, Yasmin!"

Until a few hours ago she had been for him merely a passing distraction, a new amusement to be pursued until interest waned, but now he could not contemplate life without her.

The daughter of a wandering Moorish snake-charmer, chance had thrown her across his path while travelling far north of his own territory.

Camping one night on the outskirts of a tiny village, he had idled away a tedious hour in an ill-lit café, drinking execrable coffee and watching an entertainment that, with one exception, he found sufficiently boring.

But the snake-charmer's performance struck him as unusual. The Moor himself, a grim, taciturn, giant of a man with a brutal, sinister face, had inspired him with nothing but disgust; but the girl was a new type that caught his errant fancy.

Though unveiled, and of a class that commanded but little respect, she was totally without the brazen forwardness of her kind.

Instead she carried herself with a shy, natural dignity that was oddly out of keeping with her garb and profession.

Intrigued, the next day he had endeavoured to seek her out, only to learn that she had left the village with her Father in the early hours of the dawn.

With no thought in his head but the gratification of a passing fancy, he had followed her northward, and chance meetings had developed into stolen interviews, until the end had come this morning.

Who it was that had surprised them, spirited the girl away, and made prisoner of himself he had no means of guessing.

This particular stretch of country was swarming with robber bands, any one of which would look upon him as a rich prize, worth holding for ransom.

The ignominy of his position, a position due entirely to his own carelessness, bit deeply into him.

But the thought of it paled to insignificance beside the crushing fact that he was powerless to aid her, whose life was now far dearer to him than was his own.

As the weary hours dragged slowly past, the periods of light-headedness increased, and it was during one of these that the longed-for interruption to his solitude came.

He did not hear the opening of the door.

It was a brutal kick on his aching shoulder that roused him to consciousness.

Clenching his teeth to suppress the groan that almost escaped him, he stared up with fierce defiance at his captors. And at the sight of them his heart beat with sudden violence.

For of the three men standing beside him he recognised one, and that one was the last he had expected to see.

And the sinister-faced Moor was smiling evilly as he returned his stare with eyes that were as cold and cruel as those of the repulsive reptiles he trained.

But it was the two strangers who spoke first, plying him with questions that, confused and dizzy as he was, he only half-comprehended.

Had the Moor been alone he could in some measure have understood the attack that had been made on him. But of the three the Moor seemed the least interested. It was the two strangers who appeared to be principally concerned.

Who or what were they to interfere with his

liberty, to take part in an outrage for which, if he lived, he promised they should pay dearly?

Raging, but forcing himself to silence, he studied them with grim impassivity.

Both were heavily built men, muscular and athletic-looking; one seemed verging on middle age, the other to be about thirty.

And the more he looked the more puzzled he became.

Despite their bullying attitude, he felt an undercurrent of uneasiness in their manner. And, though acting together, it seemed that they were not quite in accordance the one with the other, for they broke off their interrogations frequently to argue heatedly in a language that was unknown to him.

And it was during one of these arguments that the Moor moved for the first time.

With an oath of impatience he snatched a knife from his girdle and stooped quickly over the prisoner.

"Kill—and have done," he snarled, his arm upraised to strike.

But the others hurled themselves on him and forced him back.

"Not until he speaks," cried the elder man, with a gesture of authority. "Did I not tell you so this morning, you hot-head? Until we learn how much he knows, he lives. Bring the girl, she may have more to tell."

Ahmed lay rigid, a look of horror dawning in his eyes as a terrible suspicion flashed into his mind.

He saw the Moor shake his head, heard his growl of surly refusal.

"No, her part is done. She has told all she knows. Even with her he was close-mouthed."

Then, as the bitter truth burned into him, a cry he could not control burst from his lips.

"Yasmin," he groaned. "Yasmin!"

The Moor turned to him swiftly.

"Yes, Yasmin—Yasmin," he mocked, and spat at him. "Did you think she loved you? You are a fool who has not got enough wit to keep what you had taken! You have seen the last of Yasmin. She has done what she was set to do, and she is not for you, you dog of the desert."

His voice dropped suddenly to a low, hissing whisper.

"You want to live?" he threatened. "You want to clasp a maiden in your arms again? Then speak, or I shall make you such a thing of shame and scorn that even beasts will turn away from you in fright."

He paused as if to let his threat penetrate, his features contorted in a grin of horrible pleasure.

Then slowly and elaborately he detailed the devilish methods by which he proposed to extract the information he hoped to obtain.

And, listening, for the first time in his life the son of the Sheik knew bodily fear, a cold, numbing fear that seemed to be turning the blood in his veins to ice.

He realised that somehow he had run his neck into a noose from which there was no escape; that somehow he had become involved in a chain of circumstances that, mysterious and totally beyond his comprehension, yet threatened his very existence.

If only they would kill him! Death was preferable to torture and mutilation. And was life, after all, so precious to him, who had that day lost love and faith and the hope on which he had set his heart?

He thrust the thought from him and, rallying what strength he had, steeled his courage to endure the ordeal that now seemed inevitable.

But a reprieve came from an unexpected quarter.

The two strangers, who had momentarily drawn apart, now came forward, the younger man seeming to urge some point which the other did not receive favourably.

For, cutting short his companion's eloquence with the same curt gesture of authority he had used before, he turned to the snake-charmer and tapped him smartly on the shoulder.

"It grows late, friend," he said smoothly, "and there is much to be done tonight, as you know. There is no time now for this entertainment.

"Let him sleep on the thought of what you promised him, and it may be that tomorrow he will speak to save his skin."

A low laugh of amusement accompanied his words, and for a moment his eyes rested on the prisoner with a look of callous indifference.

Reluctantly the Moor heaved himself to his feet, his face livid with thwarted malignance, his hands twitching as if loath to leave their prey.

"A day that may dawn too late," he retorted, with a snarl of rage.

Alone, the Sheik's son could now surrender to the mental anguish that, for the moment, swamped all thought of bodily suffering, the mystery that surrounded him, and the danger that still threatened.

Yasmin, whom he had loved, and loved as he knew that he would never love again—Yasmin, whom he had spared because of that love—Yasmin had betrayed him!

With a bitter cry his soul went down into the dust, and he wrestled with an agony that seemed greater than he could bear.

Twelve hours ago he had learned what real love meant. And in that moment he had reached manhood, filled with a new understanding, a new tenderness his fierce nature had never known before.

But love had died in the horror of betrayal, and with it faith and trust had perished.

Disillusioned and embittered by the terrible experience through which he had passed, the new tenderness and the new chivalry that had come to him had gone as if they had never been.

Only the elemental savagery in him remained, urging what seemed the sole thing left to him.

His young face hardened, and the cruel lines deepened round his mouth as his thoughts turned to the vengeance that should be his—if he lived.

And, by Allah, he *would* live—live to exact full payment from those who had injured him.

As he suffered, so should they suffer. And she also! Neither her sex nor the memory of his love should save her.

Love? He sneered at himself in bitter self-mockery. He had done with love!

He would never spare a woman again, to endure the same galling humiliation under which he was writhing now.

He dragged his mind to the present. How long had he lain in the little hut? How long before the morning?

A broad streak of moonlight filtering through the window above his head warned him that time was passing, that before many hours elapsed he would have to face in reality what in imagination he shrank from.

Suddenly a trivial sound riveted his attention, but as he strained his ears to listen, a tremor ran through him and his heart began to beat suffocatingly.

For these were singularly persistent bats whose feeble squeakings rose and fell with monotonous regularity. Almost unconsciously he found himself counting the seconds that elapsed between the soft twitterings.

Five-seven. Five-seven.

Ramadan and S'rir, by Allah, using again the boyish code that often, years ago, had drawn him from his tent in a fever of excitement to join some midnight escapade the Arab lads had arranged for his amusement.

Ramadan and S'rir—how had he forgotten them?

New hope flooded in upon him, and his tired eyes blazed as he strove to give the answering signal. But his tongue was stiff and swollen and no sound issued from his parched lips.

A kind of frenzy came over him as he realised what his silence might entail.

He was convinced that his men were near. Was their devotion to go unrewarded? Had they tracked him so far only to fail for lack of the response he was powerless to give?

Was the chance of escape to be lost to him after all?

If he could only move, only make some sound that should penetrate to the other side of the mud-brick wall!

Unable to speak, unable to stir, he knew that every moment the probability of his rescue was growing fainter.

Hope had almost given way to despair when

suddenly a dark shape rose level with the window on which his eyes were fixed.

Moments seemed like hours as he waited, shaking with apprehension, hardly daring to breathe, while the rusty iron bars of the window bent and yielded to the grip of two powerful hands.

One by one the bars were silently loosened and removed, and then, bit by bit, the tiny aperture was widened until the hole was big enough to permit the passage of a man's body.

Surely it must be Ramadan; his strength was proverbial.

There was a moment's interval, a soul-sickening period of suspense that sent a hundred fears chasing through the watcher's fevered brain; then a slimmer, more agile figure than Ramadan's came, feet first, through the opening, to land with the noiselessness of a cat.

The next minute S'rir was bending over him, with a long knife in his hand.

"In Heaven or Hell, O Master." He grinned, and cut the cords that bound him.

Chapter Two

It was the hour of the siesta.

The big straggling camp of the Sheik lay wrapped in peaceful quietude that would soon give place to the military discipline that was maintained among his followers.

A fighting Clan that had risen to pre-eminence in the land, they had gone through many peaceful years hoping always for the war that never came.

Too powerful to be molested by adjacent tribes, they were feared and detested for their strength and for the strange beliefs that for generations had made them a race apart.

Unorthodox, and holding tenets that were peculiarly their own, they fostered the mystery that surrounded them.

The events of more recent years had not served to lessen that mystery. The unusual circumstances attending the birth of Ahmed ben Hassan and his subsequent succession to the leadership of the tribe had given rise to extravagant and fantastic tales that had become almost legendary in the country.

For twenty-five years he had ruled his people despotically, and for them he was still the heaven-sent leader whose miraculous coming had ensured the continuance of an ancient name.

At some distance from the main camp, half-screened by the clumps of date-palms, lay the big double tent of the Sheik.

The entrance-flaps were wide open, and under the lance-propped awning two long, lean *sloughi* hounds slept with their pointed noses resting on their crossed forepaws.

Here, too, was silence; but the solitary occupant of the tent was not sleeping.

Alone amidst the barbaric furnishings that had been her home for so long, Diana Glencaryll sat at a little writing-table, gazing dreamily into space, a half-written letter lying neglected under her hand.

The passing years had dealt lightly with her.

Still slim, and boyish-looking in the neat riding-suit she was wearing, she seemed but little older than the headstrong girl who had ridden out of Biskra some twenty years before in search of adventure.

Her smooth forehead wrinkled with anxious thought as she counted over the weeks that she had been alone. For four months the Sheik had been absent.

For four months she had watched and waited for his return, tormented with fear for his safety.

It was their first long separation, and, sick with longing for the very sound of his voice, hungering for the clasp of his arms, she had realised even more than before what his love meant to her, how much his presence was necessary to her happiness.

Four months!

She tossed the pocketbook aside with a weary little sigh.

Why had this trouble come now, just when the situation was already sufficiently difficult? Slow tears gathered in her eyes as she turned to a Moorish stool beside her and took from it a leather double-photograph frame.

Her lips were quivering as she studied intently the faces of the two sons she had borne to the man she adored. Twins, but in all ways utterly dissimilar.

Instinctively she looked first at the portrait of the second-born and best-loved son. It was an enlargement of a snapshot taken by herself, and the unconventional pose, the free, careless grace of the sitter, made the likeness seem more real, more natural.

A tremulous smile passed over her lips as she counted one by one the points of resemblance to his Father that made him so much dearer to her.

In face and figure he was the exact replica of the Sheik.

There was the same great height and arrogant bearing, the same handsome face with its cruel mouth and piercing eyes staring defiantly under close-knit brows: the Sheik as he had been when she had known him first, before love had come to soften the harshness of his expression.

Even love had not changed him much, she reflected, with another rueful little smile.

It was only for her that the stern mouth relaxed into tenderness, only for her that the dark fierce eyes kindled and burnt with the light that always had the power to make her heart throb wildly.

And as in form and feature, so also in temperament did the desert-bred son resemble his Father, a resemblance that did not always make for perfect unity between them.

Too much alike, both passionate-tempered and obstinate, strong will clashed constantly against strong will.

Though secretly proud of his handsome son, the Shiek was intolerant of the younger Ahmed's failings, which were so forcefully and painfully reminiscent of his own stormy youth.

Resentful also of the fact that his future successor, already a man in years, displayed little inclination beyond the furthering of his own pleasure, the Sheik was less lenient than he might have been and his rule was an arbitrary one.

And, perpetually in disgrace, the son was chary of showing the real deep love and admiration he had for the Father who was, to him, the *beau idéal* of what a man should be.

It was Diana who formed the buffer between these two similar and yet opposite natures. Adored by both, it was she who softened the Father's harshness, she who restrained the son's extravagance, as far as she was able.

Wayward and headstrong as he was, she knew the fundamental good that was in him, and she could make allowances where the Sheik could not.

There was only one law in the Sheik's camp, his own. He demanded implicit obedience and enforced his demands with the despotism in which he had been reared.

Was the son she loved so dearly to go through the same crushing experience she had herself suffered so many years ago?

She forced the thought from her even as it rose, dismayed by what seemed to her a disloyalty.

The Sheik was right, though his methods were severe.

There could be only one head in such a community as theirs; the Boy would have to learn, as others had learned.

But, oh, dear God, if she could only spare him the pain of that learning.

Even now she knew that should the Sheik return today, there would be cause for further trouble between them, for the younger Ahmed was absent from the camp, and that in the face of his Father's stringent orders.

Her eyes darkened with fresh anxiety; then despite herself she laughed as she remembered his impetuous entrance into her bedroom early one morning, his gay insistence that a few days' leave of absence was absolutely indispensable to his peace of mind.

And his laughing disregard of her remonstrances when he had ridden away with the two sons of Yusef, who had been his personal bodyguard since childhood.

That was six weeks ago!

Used to his comings and goings, she reasoned with herself, trying to make light of this last escapade, which was only one among many.

If only he had waited until Ahmed's return!

Ahmed! the lover-husband whose devotion had made possible the solitary life that was hers! She whispered his name with yearning tenderness as she strove to quell the fears that had become almost unbearable.

To distract her thoughts she turned to the

other portrait, the portrait of the unknown first-born son, whom she had not seen since he was a child of five years old, and whose approaching visit filled her with mingled joy and apprehension.

What would his coming bring to her?

Would he ever love her as the Boy loved her?

Would he ever know that the separation which had caused her so many bitter tears had not been of her making, ever realise what that renunciation had cost her?

She had had to let him go.

Her heart still ached at the remembrance of her parting with the tiny, solemn-eyed scrap of humanity who had been sent to England as a kind of tardy concession wrung from the Sheik by the heart-broken appeals of the Father he had never forgiven.

Determined to remain in the land and among the people where he had been born, he had sent the first-born of his twin sons to be educated and trained for the position he himself would never assume.

To be Earl of Glencaryll meant nothing to him—to be Chief of the tribe of Ben Hassan meant everything.

And to that lonely old man in England the child had come as an almost divine gift, the direct answer to fervent prayer, the fulfilment of a hope that had seemed almost unattainable.

He had lavished on him all the pent-up affection of years, and the boy had grown to manhood knowing only and caring only for the Grandfather whose love he had repaid with single-hearted devotion.

It was Diana's own face that she was looking at, it was her own eyes that were staring back at her from the portrait she was holding. It was a very different picture from the other.

This was a wholly conventional studio study of a short, fair, serious-faced young man, whose air of almost premature gravity seemed at variance with his youth.

Long and earnestly she gazed at the likeness.

What had time and circumstance made of him?

What would his coming mean to him and to the parents he had forgotten?

If only she could have seen him sometimes!

If only Ahmed could have spared her for long enough to make the visits on which she had counted so confidently!

But the tentative suggestions she had thrown out had met with flat refusals that she had found impossible to risk again.

And now, at last, he was coming, and coming only because business compelled.

Her lips twisted painfully as she recalled the wording of his last letter, colder and more formal even than the others had been, in which he had expressed no pleasure in the forthcoming reunion with his family, but had given simply a dry statement of affairs.

Not the letter of a son to a parent, but the restrained, unemotional report of an agent to an absent employer.

The old Earl of Glencaryll had been dead for nearly a year. And, rigid in his determination to abstain from any benefits that might accrue to him by his Father's death, Ahmed ben Hassan had passed over to his son, fully and unconditionally, the vast estates.

He was not interested in them nor in the big

fortune, which, even if he had not been rich himself, he would never have touched.

But certain formalities, certain points of discussion, had arisen that had made a personal interview between Father and son necessary.

Months of correspondence, pedantically insistent on the one hand and casually abrupt on the other, had ended in a meeting being arranged.

Diana's heart beat quicker as she thought of that meeting, so soon to take place.

Caryll was waiting even now, at the little town of Touggourt with Raoul de Saint Hubert, for the letter that should summon him to his Father's camp.

It was only from Raoul that she had learned anything at all of the son who was a stranger to her.

His coming had always meant news of Caryll, news of the Stately House in England where he was a frequent and welcome guest.

Through his eyes she had seen her son grow from childhood to boyhood, from boyhood to adolescence.

But of the real Caryll she knew nothing. She had had to feed on the dry husks of bare facts, while she had starved for the deeper, more intimate knowledge that had been withheld from her.

When he came, what would his attitude be?

There was so much he did not know.

It was impossible to imagine that the proud old Earl could ever have confessed to his grandson the shameful story of his own short married life, could ever have told him of the tragical happening that had lost him wife and son and left him to face long years of sorrow, remorse, and loneliness.

It seemed equally impossible to blacken the

memory of the dead by revealing now to Caryll the true reason of the estrangement between the Sheik and his Father.

Caryll must be left to think what he would, to blame the one who was least blameworthy.

There was only one other who knew the real history of the Glencaryll family, and Diana guessed that the innate chivalry that was so much a part of him would keep Raoul de Saint Hubert's lips closed, unless necessity obliged him to speak.

And in her passionate love for her husband Diana found herself almost hoping that the necessity would arise.

And she knew Ahmed ben Hassan well enough to realise that he would never refer to the subject; he would ignore the possible condemnation of his son as he had ignored the relationship he had repudiated so many years ago.

In the early days of her married life Diana had exerted all her influence to bring about a reconciliation, but her endeavours had been unavailing.

She had done all that she could do. God alone knew what the future might bring.

She sighed again and, setting the photographs aside, turned once more to the letter lying on the pad before her.

But the ink dried slowly on her pen, and no more words were added to the closely written sheets. Her letter was to Raoul, waiting at Touggourt.

She had told him of the Sheik's absence, had given him directions to find the camp, and had begged him to set out immediately. There was nothing to add, nothing that she could add.

Much as she wished it, it was impossible for

her to ask Raoul to explain the family history to Caryll.

She signed her name and directed the envelope with a cold little feeling of mental chill, fighting against a sensation of foreboding that seemed to have taken hold of her.

Angry with herself, but unable to shake off the strange apprehensions that beset her, she leaned her arms on the writing-table and buried her face in her hands.

After so many peaceful years, everything seemed to be changed, and she had a curious instinctive feeling that trouble was drawing very near to her.

It was unlike her to have misgivings. It was foreign to her nature to meet trouble halfway.

What, then, was the matter with her; why was she oppressed with this feeling of coming disaster?

Resolutely she gripped herself. What was to be would be, and no power of hers could either stop or alter it.

She would leave to the future the things of the future, and live from day to day as she had trained herself to live, fighting the foolish fears that seemed unworthy.

Already the afternoon was wearing away, and sounds of activity were echoing from the camp. Soon Gaston would be coming with her tea, and then she would go for a ride to dispel the headache that had been caused by a sleepless night.

When she returned after her ride Diana vanished into the tent to bathe and change her clothes.

An hour later she came back into the softly lit sitting-room to find Yusef waiting with the usual daily report.

Motioning him to a heap of cushions near the divan, Diana settled herself to listen to his concise, business-like statement of the day's happenings, glancing at him from time to time while he talked partly in Arabic, partly in French.

There was little left of the slim, dandified youth whose airs and graces had amused her when she had first known him.

And though ten years or more the Sheik's junior, he looked considerably older than his Chief.

Married young, and the father of two sons who were older now than he was when Diana had been brought to Ahmed ben Hassan's camp, he had acquired a stability of poise and gravity of manner that made him appear older than he was.

She kept him for a few minutes longer, asking his advice on sundry matters and referring certain difficulties to his greater knowledge and experience.

But of the prolonged absence of the Sheik she said nothing, nor did she mention the truant son who was causing her so much uneasiness.

And Yusef also, whether prompted by Gaston or for reasons of his own, refrained from bringing the names of either into the conversation.

It was as though a conspiracy of silence had been tacitly agreed between them.

But each knew what was in the other's mind.

And as if wishful to make her realise what he would not put into words, Yusef's manner was more than usually attentive, his salaam more than usually deferential when at last he took himself away.

Diana looked after his retreating figure and heaved a sharp little sigh. She almost wished that he had spoken. But, after all, what could he have said?

He knew no more than she of the whereabouts of the Sheik. It was not possible for him to criticise her son. And there the matter touched him as nearly as it did herself.

Where she was anxious, so was he—and with additional reason.

His sons were responsible for the safety of the Boy, but they had no authority and had never displayed any inclination to curb his actions.

She took a broader view of the situation than Yusef did. Whatever his parental wrath might move him to do or say, she knew that, no matter what happened, Ramadan and S'rir would not be to blame.

The Boy alone was answerable for his own misdeeds.

With a feeling of mental weariness she went to the writing-table and tore open and read the dispatch that the Spahis had brought that afternoon.

It was, as she guessed, from the Military Governor of the Sahara, about the trouble with the Tuareg. His second letter to have arrived during the Sheik's absence, it was a little more urgent, a little more strongly worded.

It was a frank appeal for help from a Chief who, though independent and acknowledging no suzerainty, was known to be friendly towards the French Government and a powerful faction in his own part of the country.

Ahmed ben Hassan's cooperation was asked, indeed implored, in tracking the instigators of the unrest that had become evident in all parts of the land, and in discovering which tribes were disaffected and which might be counted on to remain loyal to the Administration.

For some time after reading the letter, Diana sat lost in thought, her brows knitted anxiously, her eyes absently following Gaston, who was moving about the room making preparations for her solitary dinner.

The General had not minced matters. It was plain that in Paris the Ministry of the Interior was frankly alarmed.

What would a general upheaval in Algeria lead to? How would it affect Ahmed?

For a moment her face grew very white and the tent seemed to waver oddly round her. Then with an effort she regained control of herself.

She had faith in her own people. And if the worst came to the worst, and it became necessary for Ahmed to take part in operations beyond his own territory—well, God would give her strength that she might not fail him.

She read the dispatch through once more and then put it away carefully. She would not answer it tonight; she would leave it until tomorrow, for what might tomorrow not bring?

In the great wide bed where she lay alone there was no need to hide the passion of misery and loneliness that swept over her, and, burying her face in the pillow, she wept as she had not allowed herself to weep before.

She wanted him!

Oh, God, how she wanted him!

More even than that night so many years ago when he had ridden away with Raoul de Saint Hubert, and she had lain agonising on this same bed, dreading that his return would mean the end of the brief romance that had come so strangely into her life.

Then she had been only his slave, the victim of his caprice and passion.

But now she was his wife, an integral part of him. And without him it was as if some portion of herself had been torn from her; as if by some horrible physical dismemberment she had lost all vitality, all strength, and what remained was merely a quivering mutilated fragment whose only capacity was suffering.

Ahmed, her splendid lover!

She whispered his name in an agony of love and longing.

Would she ever again feel the curve of his strong arm round her, ever again hear the soft, slow intonations that once had drawn her back from the very gates of death?

She had nearly died that night, the night that the boys were born. It was only his voice that had given her strength to fight for her life.

Exhausted with emotion, she lay with closed eyes, courting slumber by every device known to her.

But still sleep would not come, and hour after hour she tossed feverishly, growing every moment more wide awake, more nerve-shaken.

The cheerful noises of the camp had long since died away. Only the rapid ticking of a little clock near her broke the stillness, and finally it became more than she could endure. She sprang up to stop it with shaking, ice-cold fingers.

She did not go back to bed. The room had suddenly become unbearable.

Slipping a warm wrap about her, she went into the outer room, where a couple of lamps were still burning, forgotten as she often did forget them when she was alone.

The tent seemed airless and hot, strangely hot

for the time of year. Perhaps it was the lamps that made it so, she reflected.

Going to the door, she noiselessly unfastened the entrance-flap, not wishing to waken Gaston, who was sleeping across the threshold, as he always did when the Sheik was away.

Then she lay down on the divan and forced herself to read.

Gradually her nerves grew calmer, the rigidity of her limbs relaxed, and she lay more restfully, ceasing to listen for the sound that never came.

Perhaps it was the change of atmosphere that soothed her. Perhaps sleep, the capricious, was nearer than she had imagined.

She was hovering on the borderland of oblivion when the sound came that roused her abruptly to complete wakefulness and sent her flying to her feet, to stand with straining ears and wide, dilated eyes.

Breathless, her hands pressed tightly over her wildly beating heart, she waited, listening until the effort became an agony.

The sound came again, the harsh protesting snarl of a kneeling camel, followed by the quick murmur of men's voices.

Then the entrance-flap was flung open and a tall figure swept into the tent.

The next moment she was in her husband's arms, laughing and sobbing as she clung to him. And holding her as though he meant never to let her go, the Sheik rained passionate kisses on her upturned face.

"*Ma mie, ma mie!*" he murmured, his deep voice trembling, his fierce eyes softening into a wonderful tenderness.

"Has it seemed so long, poor little lonely

wife? Do you think I wouldn't have come sooner if I had been able? Do you think I haven't counted the days and nights until I could hold you in my arms again? *Mon Dieu,* how I have hungered for you, Diana!"

The clasp of his strong arms was pain, but she scarcely felt it.

Her lips on his, she whispered her happiness and confessed her fears, her hands running over his broad breast as if to convince herself that he had returned to her safe and sound.

It was not until he had loosened his hold somewhat, not until her questioning fingers, slipping up inside his wide sleeve, met with the unmistakable folds of a bandage wrapped round his forearm, that her eager outpouring faltered suddenly, and she went white to the lips.

"Ahmed, you are wounded!"

He smiled reassuringly, and put her from him with a quick caress.

"It's nothing to worry about, *chérie*. No bones broken. It will be healed in a day or two," he said lightly, and turned in search of a cigarette.

"But . . . how?" She panted, her eyes jealously watching his every movement.

He seemed impatient with her insistence, and lit the cigarette slowly, inhaling a long breath of smoke with the keen enjoyment of one who has not tasted good tobacco for some time.

"I was in a tight corner, and had to make a bolt for it. Luckily, their shooting was atrocious," he said, rather shortly.

And Diana knew from experience that that was all she was to hear of the matter. It was not his way to speak of himself or to exaggerate what he considered trifles.

She followed him to the divan, where he had

flung himself down, and slipped to a pile of cushions beside him.

"Have you found out what you went to find, *Monseigneur?*" she asked hesitatingly. "Do you want to tell me tonight, or are you too tired?"

She noticed, as she saw him for the first time under the full light of the lamp, how utterly weary he looked.

He slid his arm round her, drawing her bright head closer.

For a few moments he sat silent, not answering her question but staring straight in front of him, his brows drawn together in the heavy scowl that was so characteristic of him.

At last he said, "You know what I went to find out: the origin of this strange uneasiness, this strange unrest that seems to have taken hold of the whole country.

"It has been coming for some time. It began, as far as I could learn, months and months ago.

"Everywhere I went it was the same. There seems to be some mysterious and sinister influence abroad in the land, stirring up the people for some purpose I have not yet been able to discover.

"Old hatreds are being revived, old quarrels are being renewed. But it is not only old scores between the tribes that are being raked up. It is a deliberate set against the French that is being fostered.

"I listened to wild stories that were almost incredibly fantastic. Hints were dropped of a conqueror coming from the north who would sweep away the present Administration and dominate the country as Sidi Okba ven Nafi did when he brought Islam to Algeria.

"All foreigners, and all sympathising with foreigners, are to go; and it is to be Algeria for the Algerians, not French Algerians as we understand the term, but Arabs. Suspicion is rampant, and no one knows whom to trust, whom to believe."

He stopped abruptly, his face grown set and stern.

And, almost stunned by his revelations, Diana sat with tight-locked fingers, trying to take in the full significance of what he had said. It was worse even than she had imagined.

What would come of it all?

"Is that ... all you found out?" she said falteringly.

"No. I found out enough to make it extremely uncomfortable for certain persons if the French Government weather this threatening storm.

"I have followed up clues and sifted fact from fiction until I have learned the truth—of one point, at any rate. It is external influence that is at work.

"The people are being stirred up by propagandists sent by some foreign country. I haven't got to the bottom of it yet, but I am on the track of it, and of the devils who are doing the mischief."

He spoke with an odd ring in his voice that sent a sick little feeling of dread through her.

She had got him back but only until such time as he would feel called upon to resume the dangerous work he had undertaken.

She forced the thought from her, determined to be happy while she could.

She realised from his manner that for the moment there was no more to be expected from him, that he had said all he meant to say tonight. And she was content to leave the rest until later.

It was enough that he was with her, and safe, at any rate, for a time.

And something else combined to keep her silent while he ate the hastily prepared meal that had been placed for him. Despite her happiness, she dreaded the question which would inevitably be asked before many more minutes elapsed.

He rose at last with a sigh of content, and, going to her, caught her in his arms, his dark eyes kindling as they looked down searchingly into hers.

And his whispered words sent a wave of burning colour rolling upwards to the roots of her hair. Trembling, she hid her flushed face in his breast, murmuring incoherently.

But with a soft little laugh of amusement he raised her head, compelling her to meet his passionate gaze.

"After all these years—Diana, you utter child! Have you not grown used to me yet, my wife?"

And with another laugh he let her go, and turned to extinguish the lamps. He was still smiling when he joined her in the inner room.

"Useless, I suppose, to ask why I find the tent blazing with light at this time of night! Might I humbly ask if you have been to bed at all since I left you?

"And if you must turn night into day, *ma mie,* why don't you make that lazy son of yours keep you company? I'll swear the Boy hasn't lost many hours of sleep on my account."

It was her silence, and something in her face, that banished the smile from his lips and brought back the heavy scowl that so completely changed his expression.

He flung off the ragged old burnous with a gesture of anger.

"Where is the Boy, Diana?" he said shortly,

and his face hardened as he waited in vain for her reply.

"Answer me!"

It was the old peremptory voice of command, harsh as she had not heard it for years, and her eyes filled with sudden tears as her hands went out to him in a little gesture of appeal.

"I don't know, Ahmed. I wish I did!" she cried, with a quivering sob.

He drew her to him almost roughly, kissing her with remorseful tenderness.

"For God's sake, don't cry, darling. Not tonight of all nights. I'm not blaming you. But the Boy—I warned him before I left. I made him understand that he was responsible. *Grand Dieu*, I left you in his charge!"

"But, Ahmed, he is only a boy. And there was Yusef and Gaston..."

The Sheik jerked his head angrily.

"He is a man, Diana," he interrupted with swift sternness, "and he will have to answer for this as a man. *Bon Dieu!* that he should have so little sense of honour, so little sense of decency! How long has he been gone?"

"Six weeks." She faltered, and then shuddered at the great oath that burst from him.

"Who went with him?"

"Ramadan and S'rir."

"A proper trio!" he flashed, with a rather bitter laugh. "And no other escort when he knew the state of the country? The damned young fool!"

She broke down completely then, clinging to him and sobbing unrestrainedly.

And with another smothered oath he swept her up into his arms and carried her across the room.

"Don't worry, sweetheart," he whispered,

as he laid her down on the bed. "He'll turn up all right. Black sheep always do. I ought to know, for I was a blacker sheep than ever he will be—God help me!

"And God help him when I'm done with him," he added grimly to himself as he turned away to finish undressing.

Chapter Three

The peace of heaven lay over the one and only hotel in the little Arab town of Touggourt.

In the cool, shady entrance-hall, the stout French patron, ensconced within his *caisse,* lay buried in the depth of a capacious armchair, snoring sonorously, his bald head covered with a vividly hued silk handkerchief that was wafting gently to and fro with his heavy breathing.

Upstairs, in a private room, Raoul de Saint Hubert was sitting at a large table, writing.

During the two hours that had elapsed since lunch he had not ceased work except to light a fresh cigarette, and to reply briefly to the occasional remarks made by the short, fair young man who was lying in a cane chair beside the open window.

These latter interruptions, however, had become fewer and fewer, until finally they had stopped altogether, and Saint Hubert wondered, without troubling to ascertain, whether his companion was asleep.

But Caryll John Aubrey, Viscount Caryll, was very far from being asleep.

His obstinate chin thrust out, his brows knit

in the formidable scowl that marked his only point of resemblance to his Father's family, he was mentally reviewing a situation that each moment appeared to grow more distasteful, more unpleasant.

He felt out of tune with his surroundings, hating the necessity which had taken him from the one country in which he could see any good, and where lay all his interests, and he was bitterly hostile towards his Father, who was nothing to him but a faint memory.

He grudged every minute spent out of England and shrank from the undertaking for which he was himself solely responsible.

It was not self-interest that had brought him to Algeria.

And, being here, the thing would have to be carried through, pleasant or unpleasant, and there, for the moment, the matter could rest.

Ignorant as he was of the tragedy that had wrecked his Grandfather's life, he had never guessed that his own careful training had been but one of many means by which a broken-hearted man had sought to retrieve his own early misdoings.

His upbringing had been almost unique. And from childhood, orderly and methodical, with a fastidious abhorrence of anything that was unconventional and unordinary, constant association with a very old man had strengthened his prejudices and made him grave and reliable beyond his years.

Winning no academic honours, and not particularly good at games, but universally popular as an all-round good sportsman, his career at Eton was uneventful.

Shortened as it had been by the precarious

state of his Grandfather's health, he had passed straight from school to plunge whole-heartedly into the task that was to be his life's work.

By instinct and training he was a worker. And for two years he had laboured like a galley-slave to master the intricacies of the management of the vast estates, which he had been brought up to consider as a sacred trust.

To maintain the traditions of his ancient name and to be a model landlord had been his only ambition, while sport had been his only relaxation.

And it was of this, his one amusement, that he was thinking while Saint Hubert still wrote steadily on.

Even sport seemed denied to him in this rotten country, he reflected, his mind turning regretfully to the gun-cases in the adjoining room that had remained strapped since leaving England.

With a smothered cry he got up and went out to the tiny balcony that projected from the window and stared down into the street.

"My God, what a country! My God, what a people!" he muttered wrathfully.

Swinging on his heel, he flung back into the room to ask:

"How much longer shall we have to wait in this God-forsaken place?"

There was something in his tone beyond the mere words that made Saint Hubert, looking up from his work, peer at him for a moment before answering.

"What's the trouble now, Caryll?" he enquired quietly, and sympathy and an intense understanding made him, contrary to his usual practice, utter his counter-question in English.

A faint flush crept over the younger man's

face and his angry eyes wavered under Saint Hubert's scrutiny.

"Oh, only the usual thing," he muttered impatiently.

Saint Hubert paused for a moment, looking keenly at his companion.

"I don't think you quite realise what your position is here. It is something in this country to be the son of Ahmed ben Hassan. You have reason to be proud of your Father, Caryll."

It was a quiet but direct challenge. Though he expected a retort, he was not quite prepared for the violent outburst his words provoked.

Starting as if Saint Hubert had struck him, Caryll's clenched fist crashed on the table between them and his face went livid.

"Proud—of my Father!" he cried passionately. "Proud of being the son of an Arab..."

"Caryll!"

But even Saint Hubert's stern reproof failed to stem the flood of bitterness which, pent up for years, burst out at last.

Pacing the floor now with quick, uneven strides, Caryll flung out his hand in a gesture of supreme scorn.

"What else is he?" he flashed. "And what has he ever done that I should be proud of him? Am I to be proud because he has neglected me all these years?

"Am I to be proud because he broke his Father's heart, because he let the poor old man die without seeing him? Do you think I can forgive him for that? Do you think I can forget my Grandfather's death, and his voice, at the end, only a whisper, 'My son, my son!'

"God, how it hurt! And you ask me to be proud of him! It was pitiful to see his agitation when you were coming; it was worse to watch him after you were gone.

"And, kid as I was, I used to curse the man who had made him suffer. My God, how I hated him! And do you think it has been pleasant for me, all my life, to be known as the son of 'those extraordinary people who live in the desert'?

"I wanted ordinary parents who could be produced like other fellows' people. But it isn't that that rankles so much. It's knowing myself the son of a man who . . . who . . ."

He broke down completely and dropped into a chair by the table, burying his head in his arms.

It was a frank avowal at last of what Saint Hubert had often suspected, but never before had the shy, sensitive lad raised the barrier of reserve he had built about himself and laid bare his innermost feelings.

Never before had he given the least inkling of the morbid brooding that had poisoned his young life.

And now, as he watched his heaving shoulders, Saint Hubert found himself again confronted with the problem that had troubled him for years.

Was he justified in withholding the knowledge he possessed, or was it his duty to enlighten Caryll as only he could enlighten him?

The love between Grandfather and grandson had been wonderful, and for Caryll the old man had stood as a type for all that was honourable and upright.

Must he destroy the lad's faith and sully his ideal by brutally acquainting him with the naked facts of the pitiful old story?

Once before he had had to tell that story.

But would Caryll receive it as his Mother had done? Then it had been told to justify the man who was Saint Hubert's dearest friend. And was there not the same reason now for its telling, and an even greater reason?

It was impossible that Caryll should be allowed to remain in ignorance, that he should not be given the chance of judging for himself, after he knew the actual facts, between his Father and his Grandfather.

Saint Hubert went slowly to the other side of the table.

But as he laid his hand on Caryll's shoulder he paused in frowning indecision, checking the revelation that was on the point of utterance.

Not yet. He would wait a little longer, wait until the difficult family reunion was accomplished, until the knowledge of his Mother's love and a better acquaintance with the Father he now hated should have paved the way and made the story easier for him to bear.

And, already restless under his hand, it was Caryll's husky voice that filled the blank.

"It's all right, Uncle Raoul," he said jerkily, his head still buried in his arms. "I'm sorry I made a fool of myself. Forget it, please. I just couldn't help it. I had to speak, it's been choking me for years."

He raised his head suddenly, gripping Saint Hubert's hand with a force that made the Frenchman wince.

"Why are you so good to me, Uncle Raoul? You and the old man, between you, have hardly let me realise the need of a Father, and you taught me even more than he did, much as he loved me.

"I wish I could tell you how grateful I am.

But I can't express myself. You've been more than a Father to me, Uncle Raoul—by God, I wish you were my Father!"

Behind him, Raoul de Saint Hubert stood silent, thankful that his face was hidden, struggling with a rush of emotion that almost overpowered him.

These last few words, a mere spontaneous expression of affection to the one who uttered them, held a deeper and more poignant meaning for the man to whom they were addressed.

His son, that might have been!

The living image of the woman he adored.

The thought of it was like a sharp sword turning in an open, unhealed wound. His dark eyes drawn with pain, he fought again with the undying love he had kept hidden so long, and the constant aching longing that never left him.

For twenty years he had played a part, had kept his secret, and had remained her friend.

It was Ahmed's love, not his, she had wanted. And to give her her heart's desire he had wrestled with death to restore to her arms the man who had wronged her so greatly.

And the happiness he had prayed for had come to her, and her happiness was more to him than was his own.

Even Ahmed had never guessed. Unselfish, there was no bitterness in his heart, and his friendship for the Sheik had survived the greatest test of all.

Since his outburst Caryll had relapsed into moody silence, sitting huddled on the cane chair to which he had returned.

He neither moved nor lifted his head when Saint Hubert went to the open window and, leaning against the jamb, spoke with his back half-turned to the room.

"I'm sorry I've got to leave you again, *mon cher,* but I've an appointment this afternoon. And tonight I am dining with the Caid and his son, who came to see us yesterday.

"I know you won't want to go. As the Caid has no French, I made your lack of Arabic a sufficient excuse."

His effort to ignore the previous conversation met with scant success. Still sore, and obstinately hugging his grievances, Caryll's sarcastic rejoinder was an open invitation to further discussion.

"Does my brother look like that young Arab?"

Almost at the end of his patience, Saint Hubert found his own temper rising, but amusement was mingled with annoyance.

Mentally, he contrasted the vigorous, athletic frame and healthy, handsome face of the younger Ahmed ben Hassan with the gross and debilitated figure of the young Caid, whose pallid cheeks and sensual kief-drugged eyes had made so unpleasant an impression on him yesterday.

"I haven't seen the Boy for nearly two years," he said shortly. "As I said before, why not wait until you can see and judge for yourself?

"Don't make more obstacles, Caryll. I know you are hating the whole thing. I know it is all very difficult for you. It is probably going to be difficult for them also—your people, I mean. I might also add that it is difficult for me."

Caryll's hand shot out in swift contrition.

"Why don't you kick me instead of arguing with me?" he mumbled. "I can't get used to it, and it's no good trying.

"I hate the country, and I hate the people.

You want a muck-rake for the one and a hose-pipe for the other!"

Saint Hubert laughed, and with a wave of the hand he was gone.

The hot blood poured in a dark wave over Caryll's face, and he jerked his head angrily as he stood staring at the door that had closed behind Saint Hubert.

But it was with himself that he was angry; and it was the knowledge of his own inconstancy, the knowledge of a newly awakened interest that was contrary to his vehement assertions, that was moving him so strongly.

While sincerely hating the country and its people, surely it was still possible to feel pity for one member of the race, who, different from the others, had become intriguing by reason of that very difference.

It was the vivid contrast that had compelled his attention and excited his interest.

And it was only pity he felt, the same pity that inspired him when he watched the dumb suffering of a tortured animal.

What else was she, poor little ill-used kid! His face flushed again with honest indignation as he remembered their first meeting.

It was little more than two weeks ago. He had ridden out one morning, accompanied only by his English manservant, towards Temacin, and tiring of the flat, uninteresting road, had made a detour on the return journey.

Among the deserted sand hills beyond the Tombs of the Kings he had come suddenly upon a gigantic Arab mercilessly beating a slender slip of a girl who, though silent under the terrible chastisement, was writhing with pain and fighting desperately to free herself.

Without thinking of the possible consequences, forgetful of Saint Hubert's repeated warnings, conscious only of the rage and disgust that filled him, Caryll had shouted to his man and galloped straight for them, his fingers gripping the heavy hunting-crop he happened to be carrying.

The long, pliant whip-lash had whistled through the air and coiled with a strangulating hold round the throat of the Arab, who had stumbled to his knees, dragging the crop from Caryll's grasp and releasing the girl as he fell.

He had risen in a flash, a knife gleaming in his hand, and tearing the thong from his neck had sprung forward, his face working horribly, his wild eyes almost frenzied in their murderous rage.

Spurring his horse aside, Caryll had avoided the furious thrust aimed at him, and the man had found no further opportunity.

For, crouching low in his saddle and swinging the recovered crop in his hand, the valet had come to his master's assistance, and charged the Arab deliberately, endeavouring to ride him down.

And before this second onslaught the big native had turned and fled, running with almost incredible speed, while the valet, with a joyous and ringing "Gone away!" had chased him until further pursuit seemed unnecessary.

Dismounting, Caryll had gone compassionately to the girl, who lay motionless, face downwards, on the sand.

Shy always with women, and already wondering whether his interference might not do her more harm than good, he had patted her shoulder diffidently, wishing himself a thousand miles away.

Shivering at his touch, she had sat up slowly, looking at him with a kind of strange wonder in which there was neither curiosity nor fear.

She had made no cry before, and there were no tears in the dark, unfathomable eyes that gazed into his. But a thin stream of blood that trickled from her lip betrayed the anguish she had heroically concealed.

It had stirred his admiration as it deepened his compassion.

He had stammered a few words without much hope that she would understand them.

But she had answered in fluent French, her soft voice dragging wearily, though her tone had been almost unconcerned.

"*Je m'en suis habituée.*"

She was used to it!

The rush of anger that went through him had nearly choked him. He had tried to question her, but her answers had been evasive.

And, not knowing whether to go or stay, he had lingered, wondering helplessly if, having gone as far as he had, he ought not to make some effort for her further protection, but totally at a loss how to set about it.

From time to time he had glanced at her covertly, his eyes irresistibly drawn towards her. And each time he had been struck by the uncommon beauty of her unveiled face, the childish purity of her expression, and the fresh sweetness that seemed to envelop her.

Poorly clad as she was, from the top of her bent head to the tips of her tiny naked feet she was *clean*.

It was the girl herself who put an end to this strange encounter. When the valet returned she made a little gesture of gentle but unmistakable dismissal, and for the first time murmured a few shy words of thanks.

There had been nothing for Caryll to do but

go, and he had ridden back to the hotel still wondering whether the husband, father, or lover—whichever the brute might be—would profit by a wholesome lesson or wreak a tenfold vengeance on his hapless victim.

He had been haunted by the thought of the fragile girl helpless in the hands of her brutal master.

Since then there had been several meetings, chance meetings that had come unexpectedly at various outlying districts of the town.

And always she had been as when he first saw her, unconcerned at his coming, indifferent to his going. She accepted him as she had accepted his first appearance, coldly and almost apathetically.

There was no embarrassment, no trace of girlish coquetry in her manner, and there was never any suggestion of a consciousness of sex when she talked with him; that they were man and woman alone seemed never to occur to her.

It was not what he had expected of an Oriental woman. And often he had wondered if the reason lay with himself and not with her, if his own shy *gaucherie* was the cause of her complete self-possession and the dispassionate attitude she adopted towards him.

But even her self-possession had a quality in it that was unhuman. Different from any other child or woman he had ever seen, she seemed to be lacking in vitality, seemed listless, like a creature moved only by external influence, emotionally dead.

There was a faint, stunned look in her eyes and a lifelessness in her movements that made him think of a beautiful, passionless automaton.

She never spoke much. She would sit silent

for long periods, staring dreamily into space as if her thoughts were far away, if thoughts indeed she had.

But something he had gleaned from her. He knew now that the huge Arab was her master; sometimes she spoke of him as her Father, and then, again, would calmly deny the relationship.

He also had learned about her work: once he had come upon her with a large black snake wreathed about her slim shoulders, and disgust had given place to grudging admiration as he watched her skilful handling of the repulsive reptile.

Curiosity had even been strong enough to overcome his repugnance and draw him to the disreputable Café Maure.

The Café Maure!

After dinner he glanced at his watch, wrestling with the sudden impulse that came to him, then went into the adjoining room.

Slipping an electric torch into his pocket, he picked up a hat and a light overcoat and ran hastily downstairs.

Alone in the hall, the patron was seated in his *caisse,* checking wine-slips and adding up interminable rows of figures.

He started up as Caryll appeared, and bustled forward, bowing obsequiously.

"One of the guides? In one little moment, *Monsieur le Vicomte* . . ." he began, then withered under Caryll's scowl and curt:

"No, thanks."

"But, *Monsieur le Vicomte,*" he protested, his fat hands waving in the air, "after dark it is not safe, and there has been a fracas in the streets already tonight. . . ."

But Caryll had gone, and there was no one left to hear his warning but the hotel cat.

Outside in the darkness Caryll was hurrying towards the marketplace. He did not attempt to argue the motive that was again taking him to the Café Maure.

As he went he was conscious of other hurrying figures that passed him, and he felt his way cautiously through the darkness; but at the outset he caught his foot in something, and almost fell headlong.

Recovering himself, he switched on the torch and growled at his own stupidity as he saw the beam of light flashing on the two thin steel rails stretching across the road.

He had forgotten the tiny ammunition tramway that, traversing the lane, led to the distant barrack-yard. He might have remembered it.

He had stumbled over it before, often enough!

A few steps further on was the Café Maure, brilliantly lit and in full swing already, a deafening noise of tom-toms and brazen trumpets crashing through its open door.

He stood for a moment, his gaze going past it and beyond to where lay the silent emptiness of the rolling sand dunes and the lonely road to Temacin.

Then, pulling his hat further over his eyes, he strode on, almost colliding at the corner with the solitary Soudanese sentry who was standing like a bronze statue in the angle of the wall.

The café was full tonight; fuller, it seemed to Caryll, than he had ever before seen it.

Blinking at the sudden light, he made his way across the dirty floor to the seat he usually occupied, and, pushing back his hat, lit a cigarette and surveyed his surroundings.

There were a lot of desert men here tonight, more than he had ever seen before, he thought, as his eyes ranged over the crowded room.

And full as the place had been when he entered it, it seemed to have become even fuller in the last few minutes.

There was a sudden crash of unharmonious discord before the music sank to a soft whisper, the tom-toms faint and subdued, the reedy piping of the solitary flutist coming like a far-off echo.

There followed a breathless hush, then a murmur of expectancy as a little procession filed in from the inner room.

Two Negro lads came first, solemn as little ebony statues, bearing between them a big covered basket, which they placed in the middle of the cleared space, before retiring to the foot of the dais, where they squatted, motionless, their arms wrapped round their updrawn knees.

Then *she* came, gliding slowly forward with never a look to right or left, with half-closed, dreamy eyes that seemed to see nothing, and a set, expressionless face.

Towering behind her was the evil-visaged snake-charmer, grim and repellent-looking, his huge arms bared, his naked chest half-hidden by the swelling coils of a big black snake.

It was the man who opened the performance. But, extraordinary as was his exhibition, it was only the girl he looked at. And she neither felt nor saw his earnest scrutiny.

Drawn close to the little Negro boys, she knelt on the dusty floor, listless and self-absorbed, waiting for her turn.

The applause that followed the preliminary display was interrupted by the sound of a commotion at the other end of the room. But the disturbance, whatever it was, was quickly over.

Glancing backwards, Caryll could see only that some rearrangement seemed to have taken place amongst the audience—that the desert men appeared to be more in evidence, collected densely about the entrance and spreading forward into the room in two lines, hemming in the rest of the spectators between themselves and the walls.

They were a wild-looking lot, he thought as he eyed them curiously, and probably keener on the performance than on the habitué of the café.

But his interest in them evaporated quickly, for *her* turn was coming.

Slowly she rose to her feet. Slowly she came forward to the big closed basket near which the Moor was squatting with a native pipe in his hand.

Only the tom-toms were sounding now, in a rhythmical muffled beat.

At last from the snake-charmer's pipe came a thin little trickle of minor melody, rising and falling like the sighing of the wind.

The lid of the basket stirred, fell back, then stirred once more, to slip aside, and up from its cavernous depths came a flat, sleek head with open jaws and swiftly darting tongue.

Higher and higher it rose, drawing after it coil after coil of sinuous, writhing body, looped fantastically, which swayed to the lilt of the music.

And to it went the girl, one hand outstretched, the other upraised towards the grimy ceiling.

With a soft hiss the snake turned to her, feinting and hesitating, advancing and withdrawing, till at last with a quick rush it glided swiftly up her slender arm.

Then round her shoulders it worked its way and down her other arm.

For a moment she stood rigid, holding it aloft, then with a sudden movement she shook it free, and, catching it as it fell, raised its stiff extended body in both hands high above her head.

And standing so, for the first time she raised her eyes, staring blankly at the sea of faces before her.

But only for a second.

There was another uproar near the door and a rush of white-clad figures, and Caryll, with the others, leaped to his feet, his heart thumping furiously as he realised what had happened.

The men from the desert were in possession of the room. Armed now with the rifles they had hitherto kept concealed beneath their cloaks, they stood like a living rampart round and in front of the terrified crowd.

A door slammed violently; as suddenly as it had arisen the tumult subsided, and in the silence that followed Caryll heard the sound of a woman's piercing shriek.

Sick with fear for the girl he knew all at once he loved, he tried to get to her, but an iron hand dragged him back; and writhing in the grasp of the nomads who held him, he watched with agony the terrible change that had come over her face.

The snake, forgotten, had dropped to her feet, and, alive at last, her features convulsed with horrible fear, she stood staring, staring like a thing distraught.

Mechanically his own eyes followed her frenzied stare.

It was a man she was looking at. A man who, standing erect, with his back to the closed entrance, now came slowly forward, pacing with leisurely and haughty step between the ranks of white-clad nomads who, pressing back, kept free for him an open pathway up the room.

Young and tall, and arrogant in his bearing, his handsome face was marred by a half-healed scar which, stretching midway between his silk-bound turban and his scowling black brows, gave him a strangely sinister appearance.

He walked with unconcerned indifference to the terror he inspired, his blazing eyes fixed only on the girl, who shrank and trembled at his approach.

The room was still, only the measured footfall of the unknown broke the tense silence—that and the low, continuous moaning that issued from the girl's lips as he neared her.

He reached her at last and halted, and with a wail of fear she sank to the ground, covering her face.

As he paused, swiftly between them rose the menacing bulk of the great black snake, hissing venomously and striking at him with its hideous head.

But with a cold smile of contempt he thrust it aside and turned again to the girl at his feet.

Stooping, he caught her head in his hands and forced her, half-fainting as she was, to meet his gaze.

For a long and breathless moment he stared at her.

Then he laughed, a soft, cruel little laugh that had in it both bitterness and triumph, and sweeping her ruthlessly into his arms, he flung her over his shoulder.

Terrorised or unconscious, she lay limp and

inert. And for another moment he held her so, facing the room, a revolver dangling in his slim brown hand.

There followed a moment of terrific suspense, during which his flashing eyes passed over the powerless figure of the raving Moor with a look of amused scorn, and then seemed to stare straight into Caryll's.

Then with a second mocking laugh he raised his head and, firing at the lamp above his head, leaped for the door.

And as he ran there came an answering crashing volley, and the room was plunged into darkness.

In the yelling, stamping inferno that ensued, Caryll felt the iron fingers that had never once relaxed their grip tighten on his wrists, felt powerful arms close round him.

He found himself, despite his furious struggles, drawn swiftly backwards into the little inner room, which was also in darkness, and from there propelled into the cool blackness of the night.

Careless of what happened to himself, thinking only of the girl, he fought desperately for freedom, filled with a wild desire to seek her and save her if it were possible.

But even as he struggled he knew in his heart that the thing had gone beyond his power of interference, knew instinctively that what he had seen tonight was no casual happening but a deliberate move in some chain of circumstance that was all a part of the mystery that seemed to enshroud her.

It was evident that the audacious assault on the café had been planned and carried out by one who was known to the principals concerned.

There had been recognition as well as fear in the girl's terrified eyes.

He realised that his own brief romance was over, that he was outside and beyond this desert drama of which he had touched only the fringe.

Though love had come to him, he was nothing to her. He formed no part of her scheme of existence.

And now she had passed out of his life, as strangely as she had entered it.

Even had he been free to try to find her, he knew his task would have been a hopeless one. And he was not free.

Fight as he would, his strength was not equal to the combined force of the two men who, one on either side of him, were racing him through unknown pathways, he knew not where.

He could not ask, for a rough muscular hand pressed over his mouth held him speechless.

Whoever they were, they seemed to have eyes like those of cats, for time and again they leaped aside to avoid obstacles that in the darkness he could not see.

For what seemed an interminable period he was forced onwards.

Giddy and confused, his heart knocking against his ribs, he had begun to wonder what his own fate was to be, when suddenly the men slowed down, the hand was removed from his lips, and to his amazement he found himself standing close to the entrance of the hotel.

How he had got there he could not think; it was certainly by no way he had ever been before, and, gasping for breath, he swung round to interrogate the men he knew now were friends and not assassins.

But one had already vanished, and with a

quick whisper the other seemed to melt away into the night even as Caryll looked at him.

"Tell *Monsieur le Comte* that Daoud ben Ali has paid some of his debt."

The cryptic message was ringing in his ears as he turned and stumbled into the hotel.

Chapter Four

Outside the café, the younger Ahmed ben Hassan stood for a moment in the darkness, listening to the sounds of tumult that came from inside the building.

He looked searchingly about him while he stripped the burnous from his shoulders and wrapped it round the girl's inanimate body.

A smile flickered over his lips as he gathered the shrouded little figure into his arms and glanced at the spot where the Soudanese sentry should have been, and was not.

It was too dark for him to see, but the silence that reigned in that quarter told him that Ramadan and S'rir had successfully carried out their part of the evening's work.

Gripping his slight burden closer, he turned and ran lightly in the direction of the Tombs of the Kings, as though leaving Touggourt behind him.

Since leaving the café he had seen no one and was confident that he himself had not been seen.

And the weird loneliness of his surroundings,

the solemn beauty of the starlit night, seemed strangely in accordance with his mood.

For weeks he had dreamed of what this night would mean to him, for weeks he had planned what this night should bring him, and his heart was filled with a fierce elation as he hurried through the gloom.

In spite of almost insurmountable difficulties, he had done what he had set out to do, and the first part of his vengeance was accomplished.

It was Ramadan and S'rir who had made this longed-for vengeance possible.

Without them he could have done nothing, for without them he would not even have been alive to fulfil the great oath he had sworn as he lay bound and helpless in the squalid hut where they had found him.

The memory of those ghastly hours of suffering would go with him through life. His face was wet with perspiration now as he thought of it.

He had almost given up hope, when Ramadan's broad shoulders had risen level with the little window; for what had seemed an eternity he had waited, sweating, with mingled hope and apprehension, while the two brothers laboured to force an entrance.

He had fainted outright when S'rir had cut the cords that bound his numbed and powerless limbs.

The next few hours had been a blank. He had no memory of the superhuman efforts of his men to hoist him, unconscious, in Ramadan's strong arms, while S'rir followed with his own horse, which they had found before tracking him to the deserted village to which he had been taken.

It was the pain of his dislocated shoulder being wrenched into position that had roused him. And, conscious, he had strenuously resisted his followers' endeavours to persuade him to return to his Father's camp.

He had sworn an oath, and no power on earth would have swayed him from it. And little by little he had swayed his men until their desire for revenge was as great as his own.

Day by day his spirits had risen as he had seen his triumph coming nearer; night after night, until sleep overcame him, he had lain listening to the peaceful breathing of his companions, planning his vengeance.

Touggourt had been reached at last. Unwilling at the outset to show himself openly in a town where he was known, he had waited until the dusk before entering, a few hours after the Moor's arrival.

From start to finish, the daring *coup* he had designed had gone more easily than he had ever dared to hope.

With the aid of liberal bribes lavishly bestowed, Ramadan and S'rir had found no difficulty in collecting a motley gathering of genuine nomads, and idlers willing to pose as such, who were only too eager to join in an enterprise directed merely against a wandering Moor whose religious views they objected to.

From Ramadan and S'rir, Ahmed had learned of the snake-charmer's success at the Café Maure. From them he had learned also that the girl was allowed to wander freely about the town.

But to recover her in that easy fashion had not appealed to him!

He had conceived a more dramatic and satisfying form of revenge.

Openly, and with all the show of force he could muster, he would take her back before the very eyes of the men who had used her as a decoy to capture him.

That done, and not until then, he would endeavour to trace the secret hiding-place and learn more of the movement of the strangers whose mysterious speech and behaviour had so strongly aroused his suspicions.

Mere supposition was not enough to go on; it was actual facts he wanted, a clear case that he could lay before the French authorities thereby avenging his own private grievance and aiding the Administration at one and the same time.

He had been more interested than his Father had imagined in the strange unrest that seemed to be spreading over the country, and the experience through which he had passed had set him thinking more deeply than he had ever done before in all his thoughtless young existence.

In pursuit of his own pleasure he had stumbled upon a secret that seemed fraught with sinister import, and the mad escapade he had entered into so lightly had become a desperate game that had already nearly cost him his life.

That he had been mistaken for other than he was, he had been certain from the first.

But, remembering the questions and the threats used against him, he had become convinced that chance had given him an insight into operations which up to now had been studiously hidden.

This oddly assorted trio were in some dark and unfathomable way connected with the mystery that was abroad in the land.

His startling reappearance could not fail to

warn them of their danger and put them on their guard.

But in the meantime he held them in the hollow of his hand, for unless their resources were greater than his own, they could not leave Touggourt without his knowledge.

That much he had provided for. For days and weeks he had schemed and planned, and tonight he had achieved the first fruits of his victory.

Tonight he held in his arms once more the woman he had come to hate—yet still desired.

Why did he want her?

Why did the mere possession of her seem so much more to him than the further retribution he would exact from those others whose tool she had been?

In this land of tempestuous love and primitive passions, many a woman had died for less than she had done to him. But he did not wish her dead.

He wanted her alive, that she might suffer as he had suffered, that she might know him lord and master of her destiny.

The inborn savagery of his nature was uppermost as he scowled down at her, his lips parted in a mirthless grin of pure cruelty.

He knew that she had awakened from her swoon; though she made no sound he could feel her trembling in his arms, could feel the wild beating of the heart that lay so close to his own.

She might well tremble, she who had dealt so treacherously with him! She might well fear, she who had lured him, with lies and hypocritical kisses, to almost certain death!

He had no illusions about her now, he who had been a dupe and a fool. He would never spare her again for the sake of the child-like innocence she had known so well how to assume.

He would keep her until she had learned the worthlessness of the beauty with which she had sought to ensnare him, keep her until desire faded—*et puis, bon soir!*

His face was drawn into bitter self-mockery as he halted on top of a sandy incline to look about him.

Arriving at the outer walls of Touggourt, he kept close under the shadow of the houses, making his way cautiously, his footsteps noiseless in the loose soft sand, his eyes straining through the darkness, his heart beating quicker as he neared his destination.

He met with no other midnight wanderer, and treading the empty, soundless streets, he came at last to a halt before the massive iron-bound door of the house he sought.

It opened at his soft knock, and closed swiftly behind him as he strode along the narrow, dim-lit passage that led to an open courtyard where flowering shrubs in tubs clustered round a solitary palm tree which reared its feathery head upwards to the shining stars.

Crossing the tiny tile-paved quadrangle, he passed through a small ante-room, decorated with antique firearms and hawking accessories, to a big inner room.

Arab and French furnishings of costly and elaborate design were scattered indiscriminately in a room which, luxurious in its equipment, enervating and subtly sensuous, seemed to breathe an atmosphere of voluptuous indolence.

Incense-scented and flower-filled, hung with heavy draperies and carpeted with thick Guemar rugs that deadened every footfall, it appeared, despite the luxury in which he had himself been reared, like a gilded prison to the desert-bred man who entered it.

And a prison it would be until his work in Touggourt was done, he reflected grimly.

The suite terminated in a bedroom that was reached through a narrow archway screened by silken curtains.

Smaller than the adjoining room, it was furnished in the same sumptuous fashion and contained a similar medley of Oriental and European appointments.

And in this innermost room, this prison within a prison, he set her down at last, sliding her to her feet and freeing her from the suffocating folds of the burnous.

Shrinking from the sudden light, half-dazed and trembling, she stood swaying giddily, heedless of her surroundings, her fear-filled eyes fixed on the sinister, unsmiling face that was so different from the laughing, boyish one she remembered.

Awe and wonder seemed to be contending with the terror that convulsed her features as she stared at him, her tiny hands stealing upwards to clasp her palpitating throat.

Slowly she crept nearer.

Then with a strangled cry, half-moan, half-sob, she flung out her arms and sprang towards him.

"They told me...you were *dead!*" she gasped.

But the sudden gladness that flooded her eyes faded under his menacing stare as swiftly as it had risen.

With a short fierce laugh he stepped beyond the reach of her quivering fingers.

"We do not die so easily—we of my Father's house," he answered slowly. "We live to destroy those who would destroy us. You have played your deep game once too often, little fool."

She shrank back with a gesture of bewilderment.

"What game have I played?" she faltered.

And suddenly, for the first time, she looked about her, quickly, furtively, her eyes wild and searching like those of a trapped animal.

He followed her terrified glance with a little sneering smile.

"There is no window here," he mocked. "It's a stronger prison than the one to which you led me."

Tears rushed to her eyes and she wrung her hands despairingly.

"What do you mean?" she wailed. "Oh, my lover, what have I done that you are so changed?"

"What have you done?" he echoed harshly. "You ask that? You fooled me with lies and kisses and false oaths of love till they came—they who had taught you to deceive and betray!"

With a cry of anguish she flung herself at his feet, twining her arms about him.

"I never lied to you... I never deceived you," she said, and moaned. "Lord, believe me, I love you."

"And how many times have you loved before?" he retorted bitterly. "How many men have you fooled and betrayed as you fooled and betrayed me?"

She shuddered violently, a look of incredulous horror leaping into her eyes.

"You think that?" she whispered tremulously. "You think that I betrayed you?"

Unmoved, he eyed her gloomily.

"I do not think, I know!"

Then his voice changed suddenly.

"I am not the blind fool I was!" he cried passionately. "I tell you, girl, I had time to think and remember while I lay waiting for death in that foul hole they dragged me to.

"I heard what they said when they tried to force from me the knowledge they thought I had. I knew then the value of the love you did pretend.

"I knew then why you came to my arms that morning—you who had been so modest before. Did you laugh when I spared you because of my love—the love that died when I learned of your treachery?

"By Allah, you shall laugh at me no more. As I suffered, so shall you suffer—till I tire of your suffering."

His voice was thick and shaking with fury. Shivering, she raised her head, looking at him strangely.

"Have you no mercy, Lord?" she breathed. "Have I not suffered enough already? Did they not beat me when I wept for you, and starve me when I would not yield to the Alman who wanted me?

"He swore to take me in the end, that only in Touggourt I should go free. And I ... I would have died rather than endure his passion. How could I go to him when I loved you still?"

"Loved *me?*" he flamed. "Or loved that other fair-haired stranger who was at the Café Maure tonight? Was it to talk of your dead lover that you met him in all the lonely places about Touggort?

"Does that touch you?" he sneered, as he saw her start. "Did you think to trick him also as you tricked me, to bring gain to the devil who owned you? Or did you love him—O maiden of many lovers?"

He laughed cruelly.

"I never loved him . . . I never loved anyone but you. Will you believe me?" She sobbed.

With an oath he stopped to unclench the trembling fingers that held him.

"Never. By Allah, never!"

But frantically she clung to him, her little heaving breasts strained close against his knees, her head thrown back, her tear-drenched eyes pleading.

"Lord, when I swear . . ."

"Have you not sworn before—and falsely?" he thundered; and wrenching her clinging arms apart, he swung on his heel.

Amidst the perfumed gorgeousness of the adjoining room he stood for a moment with clenched hands, breathing heavily.

Then he fell to pacing the floor, striding backwards and forwards with a slow, noiseless tread, kicking aside the gaily embroidered cushions that lay in his path, listening to the faint sound of sobbing that came from behind the silken curtains.

A blaze of anger went through him.

The little fool!

Did she think to convince him with tears and more lies? Did she think to save herself by protestations of innocence?

Did she think to tempt him once again with

the rare beauty of her face and form, to beguile him as she had beguiled him before, that he should forego his vengeance?

Was faith, so cruelly broken, to be bought again so easily?

He had given her his love, and she had betrayed him.

He had trusted her, and she had lied to him.

And now, to avert her punishment, she would lie to him again.

To him at last came Ramadan and S'rir, the former grave and serious-eyed, as was his way, the latter smiling his customary enigmatical smile.

"Any trouble?"

Ramadan shrugged slightly.

"None, Lord," he answered, with almost a hint of regret in his deep voice. "All went as you ordered, to Allah the praise. There will be some sore heads tomorrow, but none were hurt.

"There was nothing on the Moor, though he fought like ten devils. But on the elder stranger —this."

He laid a bulky pocketbook on the table.

"We left them bound in a ditch, with a knife near them. They will free themselves before the morning—Allah curse them! It would have been better to kill them, Lord. They poison the earth."

Ignoring his follower's comment, Ahmed took the pocketbook and looked hastily at the contents.

But the closely filled sheets were written in a language unknown to him; cramming them back into the leather case, he tossed it onto the table with a gesture of disgust, wiping his fingers as if he had touched something unclean.

"And the sentry?" he asked, looking up at his men again.

This time it was S'rir who answered, his smile broadening.

"He sleeps sweetly in a bed of onions, Lord." He chuckled.

For a little while longer he detained them, listening to further details of the evening's work and giving orders for the next day before dismissing them.

And for long after they were gone he sat on at the table, staring gloomily at the pocketbook lying amongst the plates and dishes.

If it contained what he was convinced it did, the sooner it was in the hands of the authorities, the better.

He had a deep inward feeling that he had foreigners, that their presence was a menace to made no mistake with regard to these suspicious the country he loved.

And to serve that country he was willing to risk something.

If this evening's affair had ended seriously, he knew there would have been only one thing left for him to do: he would have had to surrender himself to the French Commandant and face the consequences.

And if trouble did come of it, there was still time for him to come forward and make his *amende honorable*.

Meanwhile, the pocketbook should go to the Commandant tomorrow, with a covering note that could be more or less ambiguous.

And tomorrow he would endeavour to run his quarry to earth. But tomorrow was not yet.

A dull flush crept over his sunburnt face, and starting to his feet he began to pace up and down as he had paced the adjoining room an hour ago.

Up and down, down and up, his face set, his heart pounding, he strode from end to end of the narrow room.

Love was dead, but desire remained. Desire that sent the hot blood racing madly through his veins, desire that, gathering strength momentarily, was like a raging fire consuming him.

Passion-wrung, the colour faded slowly from his cheeks and he grew strangely pale under his deep tan.

His smouldering eyes ranged the room with a look almost of anguish in them, and from time to time broken whispered words burst from his compressed lips.

Once he paused by the communicating door and stood looking at it fixedly, his hands locked tight behind him.

Up and down again he went, his feet lagging now, until at last, with a groan, he dropped onto a divan, burying his head in his hands.

She had lied to him—why should he spare her? She had betrayed him—why should he not punish her?

He felt no pity for her helplessness. What gentleness had been in his composition was burnt out of him, gone with the love that had died so swiftly.

Moreover, he had sworn, and by Allah he would keep his oath!

What had she done to deserve his mercy?

She was his to do with as he would!

The hold he had kept over himself snapped suddenly. Tortured by the physical longing that all at once became unbearable, conscious only of the overwhelming need that was driving him, he went swiftly, with fiercely beating heart and throbbing pulse.

But on the threshold of the innermost room he paused, with outstretched hand, his face tormented.

Then, with a smothered oath, he dashed the curtains violently aside.

* * *

It was but little past the dawn when he left her.

Slipping silently to his feet, he lingered for a moment, looking down with weary, brooding eyes.

She was asleep at last, heavily, dreamlessly asleep, lying with a child's unconscious grace of pose, one tiny hand buried in the tangle of dark hair spread out on the pillow, the other stretched at her side, clutching the silken coverlet.

Even in sleep her face was sorrowful, her parted lips drooping slightly, the thick curling lashes that veiled her eyes still wet and matted with tears.

He bent lower, gazing at her intently. How young she looked, and how beautiful.

But what was her beauty to him now? Merciful Allah, if only he could forget!

He shivered suddenly at the remembrance of the night. What had those hours of vengeance brought him?

He had done what he had sworn to do, and the pleasure he had anticipated had been denied him.

She had paid for her faithlessness with tears and anguish, as he had promised himself she should pay, and his triumph was as the dust of ashes in his mouth.

The satisfaction he had expected seemed strangely lacking, and there was a dull ache in his heart that he could not understand.

With a half-impatient, half-bitter sigh he turned and went slowly away.

Having washed and shaved, he sat down to write the few covering lines that were to accompany the suspicious pocketbook he proposed sending to the Commandant.

It was an anonymous letter which implicated no one but promised further information. That done, and the whole made up into a parcel, he set swiftly to work to prepare for his next move.

Half an hour later, a ragged, dirty-looking, bare-footed nomad stole silently through the still-sleeping house and down the little courtyard, from which a nail-studded door gave access to a narrow winding lane that ran at right angles to the wider street onto which the main entrance opened.

* * *

To meet De Prefont had been greater luck than Ahmed had hoped for. The packet would go directly to the Commandant's hands, and his secret was safe with the sporting young Frenchman.

But his face grew gloomy again as he thought of the Frenchman's sporting jest. So it was his brother, his "precise and estimable brother," whom she had been meeting in "all the lonely places about Touggourt!"

His brother whom he had seen at the Café Maure last night!

In that moment when their eyes had met he had been struck with something in the stranger's appearance, an unrecognised resemblance that had seemed to make the fair-haired young man's face oddly familiar to him.

There was no doubt about it now! It was the

likeness to the little Mother that was so apparent.

Allah, what a complication! With a violent exclamation, he spat his cigarette into the canal behind him.

Was it for love of his brother that she had fought against him last night?

Sacré Dieu, not all the brothers in the world should take her from him—until he chose to let her go!

The house was silent when he arrived, as it had been in the morning; these servants of Sliman's, who had said he could stay there, were either very sleepy or very well trained to efface themselves, he thought as he passed through deserted rooms and empty passages on his way to the little ante-room.

It was in the overheated, overperfumed salon that he found her. And his first glance assured him that certain of his orders had been scrupulously attended to, and that S'rir's "withered old she-camel" knew her business, in one direction at any rate.

The change in the girl's appearance was almost startling.

In the poor little tawdry rags of yesterday she had been beautiful, but in the rich dress she now wore she seemed ten times more lovely.

A short, embroidered silk jacket, worn over two gaily coloured vests of contrasting colours, showed an inner garment of finest gauze, cut low, that revealed her delicate throat and the swell of her tiny breasts.

Her slim waist was swathed with the many folds of a *fouta* of striped silk, beneath which wide silken trousers reached nearly to her ankles.

Her little feet were bare, one thrust half in, half out of a minute high-heeled French slipper, the mate of which was lying not far away amidst a heap of shining rings and bracelets and jewelled chains that were scattered over the floor.

An odd look flittered across his face as he noticed the discarded trinkets.

Curled up amongst the cushions of a big divan, she made no movement at his entrance, and at first he thought she was asleep.

But as he drew nearer he saw the colour flame into her cheeks and a sudden shudder pass over her, while she seemed to shrink back closer into the soft nest of pillows.

He came to the point with characteristic abruptness, plying his trenchant questions as to the whereabouts of the Moor in a voice which, though low-toned as usual, was hard and unmistakably authoritative.

And throughout his interrogation she listened in silence, neither altering her position nor raising her downcast eyes.

She might have been deaf and dumb for all the visible impression his questioning appeared to make on her.

Her silence and her self-control exasperated him, but wonder was mingled with anger as his eyes swept her slender figure from head to foot.

He made a sudden movement towards her.

"Speak, girl," he said menacingly.

Then for the first time she lifted her head and looked at him, a look that was singularly intent, singularly penetrating.

Her parted lips were quivering, and for a moment she seemed to be struggling with words that would not come.

"You accused me of treachery," she whispered at length. "Would you have me now betray my Father?"

Her jerked his head with a snarl of impatience.

"A dozen times you have told me he was no Father of yours!"

Her fluttering lashes dropped swiftly, veiling her eyes.

"He's the only Father I have ever known," she murmured, her tiny mouth set as obstinately as his own. "You can kill me... but I will not speak."

For a moment he stared down at her in speechless rage. But for the English blood in him he would have beaten the truth out of her, and as it was he had to clench his hands to keep them from her.

Then with a harsh laugh he flung away and started to pace the room.

"You are not worth killing," he said contemptuously. "And there are other ways to make you speak."

She shivered again at the threat, and a strange look came into her eyes as she moved slightly on the divan, her hand stealing to the wide sash swathed about her waist.

Behind her long, dark lashes she watched him stealthily as he passed and repassed, and her supple limbs quivered while her muscles tightened slowly.

He paused beside her again, his face masklike with the effort he was making.

"For your own sake, girl, tell me what you know," he said more gently.

"For what purpose are these men in Algeria? What secret has brought them from their own country to seek mischief amongst the people of another land?

"What bond is there between your 'Father'

and these strangers? You can't know what trouble may come from your silence to this land that has won free from trouble at last."

"Do you think I care what trouble may come to this poor land of yours?" she retorted scornfully. "What are my Father's secrets to you, a son of a conquered race."

"What do you know of freedom, whose neck is under the heel of France—may Allah destroy her," he said, "who would enslave us as she has enslaved you!"

"But in Morocco we are free... and our women are better men than your weak countrymen, whose strength is kept for pleasures such as yours.

"In Morocco we women do not cringe when a man would do us harm. We strike... as I strike!"

The attack was launched with such suddenness that only his quick eye and steady nerves saved him.

Her highly trained athletic little body braced, she had moved almost imperceptibly to spring with the quick, noiseless bound of a wild animal, the gleaming knife she flashed from her *fouta* driving straight at his heart.

The keen point was within an inch of him when he caught her wrist with fingers of steel, jerking her violently backwards.

And as she reeled, his arm closed swiftly round her, gripping her quivering body till she wondered if her ribs would crack under the merciless pressure that seemed to be crushing the very life out of her.

Gasping for breath, she stared up at his livid, passion-distorted face, while slowly and cruelly he tightened his hold on her wrist until the pain of it was more than she could bear.

A low moan broke from her as her hand unclosed, dropping the knife, which fell with a soft thud onto the carpet.

For a moment she braved him, her wild eyes fixed on his.

Then, all at once, her strained muscles slackened, and with a cry of utter despair she went limp in his arms, weeping as he had never heard a woman weep before.

But the sight of her tears did not move him, and with a terrible laugh he flung her to the rug at his feet.

"Allah have mercy on you, little fool," he cried furiously, "for you shall have none from me."

She heard the crash of the door as it slammed behind him, and for long after he was gone she lay where she had fallen, writhing and moaning in an agony, sobbing as if her heart would break.

She had schemed his death, he whose life was more precious to her than her own.

If she had hurt him, if she had wounded him, her master, her Lord!

What if he had been cruel? All men were cruel. And was she not his to do with as he wanted?

And whatever he did, she could only love him, love him until the madness that had come to him, too, passed, and his love turned to her again.

Someday he would know that she had not lied to him, that she had never known that her footsteps had been tracked that morning she had gone to him, that she had never known the treachery intended that had made her seem so false.

Just now, in her madness, and to anger him, she had feigned to know more than she really knew, and let him think she held the key to the knowledge he desired.

But the Moor's hiding-place was all she could tell him . . . that, and nothing more. For what had she to do with the secret workings of the man who had ill-used her from babyhood?

His image was mixed with dim, faint memories that were like shadowy dreams of a time when gentle hands had touched her and a sweet, sad voice had crooned the half-forgotten lullaby that still fitfully haunted her.

And what also had she to do with the brutal Arab-speaking Alman whose lustful eyes had filled her with sick terror?

Because of some curious feeling she could not define, she would not betray them, but they were nothing to her, for she had lived only as a slave amongst them.

She had endured a life of misery and revolt until he, the strange lover whose magnificence had dazzled her, had come to open her eyes to love.

And for those few short hours of happiness he had loved her too!

Face downwards on the thick soft rug, she prayed, weeping until she had no more tears to shed, until broken and spent with emotion she lay exhausted, her tired brain throbbing, her weary little body bruised and aching with the violence of his powerful hands.

Did life mean nothing but suffering? she wondered, as her mind turned slowly to the past weeks of agony that had seemed to her like a living death, that had made of her a thing insensible to everything but the memory of the joy that had been torn from her.

Callously they had told her of her lover's fate, and her frenzied sorrow had only provoked their anger.

And as day succeeded day she had lived with only one thought, the hope that soon she too would be beyond the cruelty of the human fiend who had tortured her even when she was a helpless child.

She had always feared him, always shrunk from him with an instinctive feeling of horror and loathing.

But hatred she had never known before had come to her when he had lied, boasting of the deed that had broken her heart and made her see him stained with her lover's blood.

Her lover!

A great sob shook her.

No lover would have done what he had done to her last night. His love was dead. And when he came again...

Shivering, she dragged herself to her feet and stood looking about her sorrowfully, panting with the little shuddering sighs that still escaped her lips.

When he came again, love would give her strength to bear whatever he might choose to do. For nothing now could kill the passion that was burning like a living thing within her.

Her sad eyes, roving listlessly, passed over the scattered jewels she had scorned to wear, till they rested at last on the knife he had left lying on the rug where she had dropped it.

With a moaning cry she snatched it up and hurled it with all her strength into a far corner, then stumbled to the divan and fell prostrate, burying her face in the cushions.

Chapter Five

"The last camp, *mon cher*."

To Caryll, sitting moodily on a hummock of sand, with his back turned to the morning wind, Saint Hubert's voice sounded almost aggressively cheerful.

He was not by any means feeling cheerful himself. Since the day they had left Touggourt he had found the journey tedious beyond expression.

And to cap his dissatisfaction, there was the memory of that futile exhibition of a few days ago, when fifty or so of his Father's tribesmen had arrived to relieve the escort that had come with them from Touggourt.

It made him go hot and cold again now as he thought of it.

A proper fool he must have looked, with a horde of maniacs galloping all round him, yelling and blazing off their rifles.

A ridiculous waste of ammunition. Honour to his Father's son—Good Lord! He could cheerfully have done without the distinction.

Caryll's thoughts kept returning to that disastrous night in Touggourt.

Touggourt!

He drew his breath in sharply.

The little Arab town he had hated would always from now be connected in his mind with the brief romance that had flashed like a streak of summer lightning across the calm horizon of his placid existence, stirring him to a depth of feeling of which he had not known himself capable.

For the first time love had touched him, the strange, incomprehensible love of a man for a woman, and for a few short weeks he had surrendered to emotions and impulses that were totally foreign to his nature.

It had been very real to him then, though now it was beginning to seem like a wild and improbable dream.

But wild and improbable though it might be, and faintly ashamed as he was now of the deep impression the girl had made on him, he knew that he would never forget her.

Though he might love again, the memory of his first love would go with him always—a half-sad, half-tender recollection that would haunt him even as the girl's face still haunted him.

Where was she now?

What had been her fate at the hands of the devilishly handsome, sinister, smiling young desperado who had abducted her?

Had she gone to gilded imprisonment, to be petted or ill-treated at the whim of her captor, or had she already been flung aside, like a discarded toy, to join the ranks of similar unfortunates?

He winced with the horror of the sudden thought.

Circumstances had prevented him from raising a hand in her defence, and when he reached the hotel Saint Hubert had not returned.

The next morning, while concealing his own feelings, he had tried to interest Saint Hubert in her fate. But Saint Hubert had countered his suggestions for instigating a search for a missing dancing-girl.

It was impossible, he had said, that Caryll could be mixed up in an affair of which he had been merely an uninterested spectator; an affair, too, that was causing the authorities much annoyance and uneasiness.

These things happened, unfortunately, he had assured him, and Algeria was not England.

"And *noblesse oblige, mon ami*," he had concluded. "It is not for you to concern yourself with the amours and abductions of café-girls of doubtful reputation."

Saint Hubert's reasoning had brought back to him again the remembrance of inherited duties and responsibilities, and the clamouring of youthful love had gone down before the training of years.

It had all been a piece of romantic folly, a preposterous dream that could never have been more than a dream.

Even had her nationality not been an insurmountable barrier between them, it was not from the vicious atmosphere of the Café Maure, or the unsavoury streets of an Arab town, that he must choose the future Countess of Glencaryll.

But if only he could have done something to help her, something that would have lessened the feeling of shame and disgust he had for himself now!

His face flushed dully, and he turned his head away, raking the sand with nervous, impatient fingers.

"Has anything more been heard of that—café business, Uncle Raoul?" he asked jerkily.

"The row at the Café Maure?" Saint Hubert answered. "No, nothing much, at least up till the time we left Touggourt. Colonel Mercier had a mysterious packet of letters sent him which may have some bearing on the affair, but they were forwarded to Headquarters, so I didn't hear what they were.

"The snake-charmer who owned the girl disappeared in mysterious fashion, and the general idea now seems to be that it was only a private quarrel between him and the girl's abductor.

"The astute young gentleman himself has also vanished, and all efforts to trace him or secure information about him have failed. He was either really a stranger in the town, or he has been very loyally screened.

"Nobody would admit to being at the café that night, and the whole of Touggourt professes a charming and child-like ignorance of everything that occurred.

"However, it will be interesting to see if anything comes of it. In the meanwhile, if you are ready, it's about time we made a start."

It was with a feeling of pleasure not unmixed with amusement that Saint Hubert watched Caryll's capable handling of the beautiful but difficult-tempered horse that was the Sheik's first present to him.

Had Ahmed some ulterior motive in sending this particularly intractable animal? Was it to test capabilities of which he was ignorant, to see of what sort of stuff this unknown son was made?

Saint Hubert's lips curved in a little smile of satisfaction.

In whatever way Caryll might otherwise fail to win his Father's approbation, his horsemanship at least was beyond reproach.

He could ride, and that went for something in this country.

Saint Hubert was aware of an odd feeling of responsibility as he rode by the side of his adopted nephew.

In his own way, but for very different reasons, he was as nervous as Caryll in view of the meeting that would take place before many more hours were past.

His thoughts veered suddenly. Much as he longed to help him, Caryll's difficulties had taken a secondary place in his consideration this morning.

He had another, more intimate difficulty to contend with.

It was two years since he had seen her, two years since he had last deliberately tortured himself with the sight of her perfect contentment.

It was hard to look at happiness through another man's eyes, hard to witness that ideal comradeship that made the sense of his own bitter loneliness so much more acute.

But how much greater would have been the misery of his life if the Sheik's love for the woman he had taken so violently had waned, as once he had feared it would wane. That would have been a hell beyond endurance.

But Ahmed loved her, passionately, tenderly, as Saint Hubert did himself, and his own sacrifice had not been in vain.

But it was only to a man like Ahmed that she could have surrendered.

As he could not have won her himself, he would rather that Ahmed had her than another.

He drew himself straighter in the saddle, forcing back a rising sigh as he prayed again for the strength that had never yet failed him.

After all, he had much to be thankful for. She was happy, and nothing mattered but her happiness. And surely he was too old now to be crying like a child for the moon!

A smile of self-mockery lightened the melancholy of his face, and he turned to Caryll with a cheery remark.

The morning wind had died away and the day gave promise of great heat.

The immense stretch of desolate loneliness on which he was looking stirred him at last to voice the question that had been hovering on his lips for days.

"How has she ever been able to endure it, Uncle Raoul?" he burst out. "My Mother, I mean. How has she ever stood this appalling loneliness, this perfectly horrible desolation?"

Saint Hubert shrugged.

"It doesn't impress everyone that way," he answered slowly. "It has a very great fascination for some people—myself, for instance.

"Your Mother fell in love with the desert years ago, and for her its charm outweighs its discomforts. And if she did not love it for itself, she would love it for what it means to her."

"But she must have had to give up so much," objected Caryll. "She must have had to—to—sacrifice a lot to—to . . ."

He broke off with a sudden snort of indignation.

"Good heavens! A man has no right to make such demands of a woman!"

Saint Hubert shrugged again.

"But if the woman wishes it too," he countered. "And in this case she did wish it, and has never regretted it."

Caryll looked at him with a puzzled frown.

"She must be rather wonderful," he said almost shyly.

Saint Hubert met his gaze without flinching.

"She is wonderful," he said quietly.

It was during the midday halt that Caryll spoke of his Mother again.

"It's rather an odd sort of feeling," he began hesitatingly, "not to know what one's own Mother even looks like.

"I don't remember her at all, and the only photograph I have is of a curly-headed boy in breeches. She can't look like that now, you know. It must have been taken a very long time ago.

"I suppose she has changed a good deal. Of course she must be—must be..."

He paused awkwardly, his face crimson with embarrassment.

Saint Hubert eyed him with a faint smile. Was Caryll, with his precise and old-fashioned notions, going to be shocked at the youthful appearance of his Mother?

Was that very youthfulness which constituted one of her greatest charms to be a cause for further grievance to this critical and already prejudiced young man?

"She is not quite a Methuselah," he returned dryly, "though of course life in the desert sometimes has a very ageing effect on women. Some of those wrinkled old ladies we saw in Touggourt were probably years younger than your Mother."

And Caryll, lying prone and idly raking the sand, heard only the seriousness of his tone, and did not see the amusement dancing in his eyes.

"Oh!" he said, rather blankly.

And Saint Hubert did not enlighten him.

The midday halt was briefer than usual, and they had been riding for about an hour when, all at once, Caryll saw, still a long way off, a rolling column of dust that seemed to be coming rapidly towards them.

His throat went suddenly dry, and the involuntary nervous pressure of his knees made his high-spirited horse bound violently.

Dragging him down, he turned to Saint Hubert with a hoarse word of enquiry.

The Count was also peering intently ahead.

"Too far off yet to be certain," he answered, "but I expect it is your Father."

And for the first time in his life Caryll was seized with an odd kind of panic.

The dreaded meeting actually upon him, he would have given more than he cared to define to be able to turn tail and bolt in the opposite direction.

What would this Arab Father of his be like?

He had rehearsed this meeting in his mind many times, and he ransacked his brain to recollect every one of the elaborately thought out, carefully prepared speeches, but his mind seemed a dense and hopeless blank.

And all the while the column of dust rolled steadily on.

Then, gradually, it appeared to eddy and lift, to drift slowly backwards, disclosing a little band of Arabs galloping with customary recklessness, a solitary horseman riding a few paces in front of them.

For a few minutes Caryll clung forlornly to the hope that perhaps the moment had not yet come, that these might be other Arabs than the ones they were expecting.

But the wild shout that rose suddenly from the escort behind him made him realise that the respite for which he had hoped was denied him, and a queer sensation that was nervousness mingled with excitement rippled up and down his spine.

Saint Hubert had signalled to their own troop to halt, and, wrestling with his excited mount, Caryll glowered at the rapidly advancing horsemen, the admiration he would otherwise have felt swamped in the angry prejudice that made him view them with critical disdain.

They were a magnificent-looking lot of men, superbly mounted, and they could ride, he admitted to himself grudgingly.

And they would stop presumably with the same horrible abruptness that characterised all these merciless riders, regardless of the abominably cruel strain on their horses.

That one in front must be his Father—his Arab Father. The native dress, even though he was prepared for it, gave him a kind of shock, and again the odd sensation of chill rippled up and down his back.

Dismounted now, he stood with his hands thrust deep in his jacket pockets, his heart pounding furiously.

The sudden crash of musketry made him start, and his face hardened as he listened to the wild uproar of shouts and rifle-shots.

His lips curled again as the oncoming troops stopped suddenly, as he had known they would, dust and sand swirling beneath the horses' feet.

Another deafening uproar arose, mingled with the shrill screams of excited stallions, the jingle of accoutrements, and the sharp crackle of rifles.

Only the leader dismounted.

And, as if rooted to the ground, Caryll watched the tall, picturesquely clad figure swing down from the big black horse and walk slowly towards them.

So this was his Father—this was the Earl of Glencaryll!

An Arab of the Arabs!

An Arab, moreover, whose dark, handsome face was strangely familiar to him.

It was not early recollection, it was a more recently seen likeness, a likeness that seemed to carry with it the remembrance of something sinister.

Where had he seen that face before? He was still puzzling when Saint Hubert's warning touch recalled him to the present, and he turned a face that was white and strained in response to the Frenchman's urgent whisper.

"For God's sake, go first, Uncle Raoul," he said thickly.

And as Saint Hubert started forward, he pulled himself together with an effort, and followed in an agony of shyness and constraint.

The two old friends met as Frenchmen. And watching their enthusiastic greeting, Caryll shivered with disgust, swallowing nervously. Would it also be expected of him?

His short, slim figure drawn up stiffly, he stood with set lips, rigidly awaiting the ordeal.

But the Sheik made no such demands on his English son. Turning to him with a grave smile, he stretched out a slim brown hand of welcome.

"*Enfin, mon fils,*" he said in his deep, soft voice. "*Soyez le bienvenu.*"

The genuine feeling in his tone and the warmth of his firm hand-clasp were all that any son could have desired.

But Caryll was conscious only of the language in which the hearty greeting had been spoken, and the resentment he had tried to conquer welled up again irresistibly.

Saint Hubert had warned him of his Father's prejudice against the country he refused to recognise, had warned him of the Sheik's unwillingness to speak the mother-tongue with which he was perfectly acquainted.

But surely in this case an exception might have been made. Surely, in this one instance, prejudice might have been laid aside.

He had been prepared to meet his Father halfway, to sink his own prejudice as far as possible, but this French welcome was like a slap in the face.

He was going to make his own sympathies clear from the start. But speech did not come easily, and the colour flamed into his cheeks as he returned the pressure of the muscular fingers that were holding his in a grip of steel.

He had a sudden curious impression of inferiority, a feeling that, obstinate as he knew himself to be, he was face to face with one whose determination was even greater than his.

Tongue-tied, and furious at his own *gaucherie*, he found himself stammering like a veritable schoolboy.

"Thank you, Sir," he muttered awkwardly. "I'm very glad to come."

He flushed deeper as he realised the lie that had somehow been forced from him. And the quick gleam of amusement that flickered momentarily in the dark, penetrating eyes that were looking at him so intently did not tend to soothe his ruffled feelings.

But the Sheik seemed not to notice the lack of spontaneity in his son's reply, or the coldness of his tone.

"We must not keep your Mother in suspense any longer," he said with the same grave smile as before. "She has been counting the days, almost the hours, I think, waiting for your coming."

And again Caryll felt as if the piercing dark eyes were reaching to the innermost recesses of his soul, and his own eyes flickered with nervous embarrassment.

"I hope she is well," he said falteringly, and wondered miserably why even this trivial and most natural remark was so difficult to utter.

"She is always well—to Allah the praise," replied the Sheik, with a quick involuntary gesture that Caryll did not understand.

And it was not until they were mounted again, well on their way, that he conquered his shyness sufficiently to thank his Father for the horse he was riding.

From the start he had been acutely conscious of the critical eyes watching him, and, good horseman though he knew himself to be, the close scrutiny was trying to his overstrung nerves.

He had even begun to wonder if, the standards being different, he had failed to come up to expectation in this, the one thing he could do well.

And quite suddenly, to his own amazement, he found himself almost passionately desiring the approval of this man he hated. The realisation of it staggered him.

Why did his Father's approval or disapproval matter to him? Why should he care one way or the other?

But, despite himself, he knew that he did care
—cared so much that the Sheik's nod of approbation that accompanied his quiet: "I am glad you
like him; Raoul told me you could ride," sent a
most unaccountable feeling of pleasure through
him.

He rode on, marvelling at himself, angry at
his own inconstancy, angry at the curious satisfaction the few short words had given him.

The sun was setting when they reached their
destination.

To Caryll's unaccustomed eyes the camp
looked immense, the whole scene strange and
more picturesquely beautiful than anything he had
ever imagined.

Moved to unwonted appreciation, his matter-of-fact mind forgot, for once, to criticise and
condemn.

The discharge of rifle-shots that heralded
their approach passed almost unnoticed, and the
hoarse roar of cheering brought, this time, no
cloud to his face. He forgot that he was the
cause of all this tumult.

Transported out of himself, it seemed to him
as if he were gazing at some wonderfully realistic
theatrical performance, or looking at some marvellously painted and animated canvas.

With a dream-like feeling of unreality, he
rode between the Sheik and Saint Hubert through
the long lane of mounted Arabs who, drawn from
various outlying camps to do honour to their
Chief's son, stretched far out into the desert like a
living avenue.

Then on past numerous clusters of low tents,
past the noisy crowded camel-lines, past row after
row of picketed horses.

Now the deep-voiced shouting of the ranks of

the densely packed tribesmen was almost drowned by the shrill clamour of their closely veiled women and the high-pitched shrieks of the pushing, tumbling swarms of excited children.

An almost royal progress, a royal welcome that stirred some long-forgotten remembrance within him, that made his breath come short and quick.

On, with a strangely beating heart, till they reached the open space and, wheeling, faced the big, lofty tent before which stood a bright-haired, slender woman.

And wonder and amazement came as he stared at the youthful-looking, white-clad figure. Was this his Mother—that *girl!*

Then Uncle Raoul had been pulling his leg!

Indignantly he turned to him, muttering reproachfully. But there was no amusement in Saint Hubert's eyes, and his face was oddly strained and white.

"Go on, Caryll," he said huskily. "She has been waiting for you for fourteen years."

Chapter Six

"Are you pleased with your new *daughter, ma mie?*"

There was a drawling note of amused contempt in the Sheik's voice that made his wife wince.

For a few moments she did not answer but continued steadily brushing the heavy mass of shining hair which, boyishly cropped no longer, hung round her like a golden cloud and screened her face from the eyes that were watching her with lazy intentness.

Ten minutes before, he had sauntered in, well-groomed and immaculate, from the adjoining dressing-room, and since then he had been stretched out indolently on a divan, smoking in silence, waiting while she dressed for dinner.

A slow smile gathered on his lips as the moments went by and she made no reply.

Settling his long limbs into an easier position, he flicked a curl of flaky ash from his cigarette and spoke again, more drawlingly than before.

"I asked you a question, Diana."

She faced him then, tossing back the mane of bright hair with a quick, almost nervous gesture.

"Ahmed... you're not fair," she said reproachfully.

"No?" He laughed softly. "Well, at any rate, you will admit that he is at least—lady-like. Much more lady-like than you were at his age, by all accounts."

She flushed, but smiled despite herself.

"Why do you think he is not manly?" she asked. "You admit yourself that he can ride, and Raoul says he is a wonderful shot."

"So are you, my dear," returned the Sheik dryly, "and you can ride as well, probably better, than our gifted son. Your qualifications are hardly adequate. Riding and shooting are not everything. I want something more than that—something which, up to now, I have not seen in him."

The covert disappointment in his voice brought tears to her eyes.

"You haven't seen very much of him yet," she murmured; "you can't judge him after only twenty-four hours. He is dreadfully shy, and everything must be so strange and different from what he has been accustomed to.

"If he were just an ordinary guest it would be so much easier. But because he is what he is, because he can't be expected to know the reason for that horrible separation, it must be as... as difficult for him as it is for us."

She sighed.

"He only sees the one side," she went on," he doesn't know all that led up to it. He loved the old man, and we are nothing to him. He can't possibly know that I... we... that we want his love."

Her voice broke on a sharp sob that sent the Sheik to his feet and across the room in a couple of hasty strides.

Woman-like, she had wandered from the main argument to voice, unconsciously, a disappointment which in its way was as great as his. And her distress made him forget his own annoyance.

Gently he raised her bent head.

"Tears, Diana?" he chided, with a half-tender, half-whimsical smile.

And lifting her suddenly, he carried her back to the divan.

"Oh, bother dinner!" he ejaculated in answer to her remonstrances as he sat down and drew her closely into his arms.

"What does dinner matter when I've made you cry?"

She drew his head down, her eyes very wistful and pleading.

"Be kind to him, Ahmed, and try... try to understand his point of view. It must be so different from ours.

"He is not like the Boy, who has never known anything but this wild life we lead. His own life must have been so regular, so orderly.

"And living always with a very old man has made him quiet and reserved. We know from Raoul how your Father trusted him, how much responsibility was thrown on him—far too much responsibility for so young a boy.

"And Raoul says that the last two years, when we knew your Father might die any minute, his devotion was extraordinary. He gave up everything for him. And it can't always have been easy.

"Promise me, oh, promise me, Ahmed, that you'll be gentle with him, as you are gentle with me. For he is more my son than yours, I think," she added with a tremulous smile.

But the Sheik shook his head.

"I doubt it. He has got your face, my dear, but there the likeness ends. I can see no other point of resemblance."

"But, Ahmed, you'll promise..."

"I'll promise anything, in reason, that will dry the tears in those lovely eyes," he interrupted quickly, "but I can't promise to perform the impossible.

"Caryll is hide-bound in his prejudices, and appears to have come prepared to make things as difficult as possible. The concessions will have to be mutual.

"If I am to make allowances, so must he. And, to put it mildly, his attitude today has hardly been conciliatory."

"I know," she said sadly. "He seems to be on the defensive the whole time. He gives one no help, no opening. It's like trying to get inside a stone wall... and, oh, Ahmed, I *want* to get in! I *want* to make him love me. It hurt me so to let him go; even you don't know how much it cost me...."

She broke off with a sudden sob.

The Sheik's own eyes were dim as he stroked the bowed head tenderly.

"Don't I?" he murmured, with a twisted smile. "Diana, I have always known. But speaking of it would not have made it any easier. It was hard for me, too.

"But it had to be, and the result was inevitable. I knew that in sending him we were probably parting with him for always. But what else could I have done? He had to go."

For a little time she lay still, wrestling with the emotion to which she had given way, and forcing back the tears that still threatened to fall.

Then, as if stirred by a sudden impulse, she

moved in his arms and sat up, pushing the heavy hair from her forehead and looking at him with wet eyes that were full of timid entreaty.

"If only he could be told," she said falteringly, her fingers plucking nervously at the folds of his burnous.

But she saw refusal in his face even before he spoke.

With a negative shake of the head he rose to his feet, putting her from him gently.

"Impossible, Diana," he said, and she knew the accent of finality in his voice. "Neither you nor I can tell him."

Years before she had learned the futility of argument, so she made no further effort to persuade him, keeping silence while she watched him leave the room.

They could not tell him ... no; but Raoul could. And yet, how to ask him?

* * *

Not very far away, in one of the luxurious guest-tents that had been pitched on the quiet desert side of the Sheik's own tent, removed from the bustle of the main camp, their son was sitting at the same moment moodily waiting for Saint Hubert.

Already dressed for dinner, he had just dismissed his man.

Last night, during dinner and for the subsequent hours, he had been acutely aware of a sense of aloofness, of an embarrassment that had augmented his shyness and reduced him to almost complete silence.

Despite all attempts to draw him into the general conversation, he had felt himself to be the odd man out. And a common topic of conversation had been difficult to find.

Burning with resentment, he could not speak of the English home he loved so dearly, and of Algeria he would not speak.

Sensitively alive to the fact that he was unable to disguise his own emotions, the Sheik's calm, impassive features filled him with a kind of unreasonable fury.

What was hidden under that suavely courteous exterior? What lay behind that stern, inscrutable face?

Twenty-four hours ago he had asked himself these questions. Now he knew, or thought he knew.

"What is it, Caryll?" Saint Hubert said, dropping onto a chair and coming to the point with characteristic abruptness.

"No need to tell me that things have been going badly; I have seen that for myself all day. We have always been frank with each other. Be frank with me now. What is the special trouble?"

"*Special* trouble?" he retorted. "Good God, it's *everything*."

It was an echo of his first outburst in Touggourt, and Saint Hubert shrugged his shoulders with a touch of impatience.

"That's generalising," he said quickly. "You will have to be more explicit if I am to help you at all. I know you hate the country and came prepared to dislike everything. But since you are here, can't you lay aside your prejudices for the time being, and make allowances?

"Don't alienate the affection they are prepared to give you. Unhappy circumstances obliged them to part with you when you were a child, and don't forget it was for your own good you were sent to England, not theirs.

"Such a sacrifice surely demands consideration from the one who benefitted by it. Try and meet them halfway, as they have met you. You can't complain of your welcome. Your Mother's happiness at your coming is too obvious to need comment, and your Father..."

Caryll wrenched round violently, his eyes blazing.

"Don't speak of him!" he cried. "My *Father* —*God,* when I think of what I saw this morning..."

And as if speech were forced from him, he poured out in rapid broken sentences the story of the early-morning occurrence—how he had seen his Father beating a man.

"Beaten like a dog," he gasped in conclusion, his voice shaking with passionate abhorrence, "and blood—blood all over him..."

He broke off with a shudder, burying his face in his hands.

There was a long silence in which only the sound of his heavy breathing was audible.

And rolling between his fingers the cigarette he had forgotten to light, Saint Hubert looked at him with compassion.

Never had he found himself so difficultly placed; never had so much seemed to depend on his choice of words.

For the first time in his sheltered young existence Caryll had been brought face to face with the stern necessities that were indispensable to the ruling of a turbulent community that was outside civilisation.

"I am glad you have told me," Saint Hubert

said at last. "It makes it possible to understand what has been inexplicable to me all day.

"It is unfortunate that you should have seen this. This is a primitive country, *mon ami,* where passions run high and licence abounds, and there are certain offences that call for drastic measures if any sort of discipline is to be maintained.

"Here it is only the strong hand that rules. Equity and justice have to be interpreted according to the needs of the various classes of society, and the justice your Father administers is the justice that is recognised and understood by the people he governs.

"His people fear him, but they also love him as few Chiefs are loved. Did you see any signs of dissatisfaction in the camp today? No. Then isn't that a proof of what I am saying?

"If his people love him, why can't you? Believe me, Caryll, he is worthy of your confidence and esteem. How else has he kept your Mother's love all these years? And you can see for yourself that she worships the ground he walks on.

"How can you, after only twenty-four hours, know him so much better than we do?

"What if I prove to you that this hatred you have nourished all your life is unfounded? What if I prove to you that in condemning him on insufficient grounds, you have done him great wrong and injustice. . . ."

Saint Hubert pulled himself up short.

In the enthusiasm of the moment, in his earnest desire to bring Father and son together, he had said more than he had meant to say, had been almost on the point of prematurely revealing the story he had determined must sooner or later be told.

But there was no time to embark on that story now, and already he regretted the impetuous words that had escaped him.

With a muttered reference to the lateness of the hour, he made a movement to rise. But a hand on his arm arrested him.

"What do you mean, Uncle Raoul? What are you hinting at?"

The strained anxiety in the hoarse young voice made Saint Hubert wish passionately that it were other than he who must open Caryll's eyes to the truth and cause him the pain that must come from a shattered delusion.

The tragic history of his little Spanish Grandmother could not fail to touch him.

But, English to the backbone, would he ever be able to comprehend the Sheik's agony of mind when he had discovered himself to be an alien in the land of his birth and not the true son of the old Arab Chief whom, until he had reached manhood, he had thought to be his Father?

These doubts were racing through Saint Hubert's brain as he disengaged himself and stood up, his hands dropping gently on the younger man's shoulders.

"I can't tell you what I mean now," he said. "I did not intend to speak of it tonight. You will have to wait, and trust me. It is a long story, and an old one, but in justice to your Father you will have to hear it.

"What he will not tell you, I must. Your attitude leaves me no other alternative. But you will have to wait for that story.

"In the meantime, for your own sake, Caryll, I beg of you to make a fresh start. Don't let your natural good sense be warped by prejudice. Try to remember that there are other points of view besides your own."

For a moment longer he waited, looking down on the set, averted face, then his hands fell to his sides and he moved towards the door.

Very slowly Caryll followed him, but it was not until they were standing outside the tent in the white moonlight that he spoke.

"I'll try," he said drearily, "but you're asking rather a lot of me, Uncle Raoul. And you've hinted at something, something connected with the mystery that has always hung over our family.

"If you have to tell me, I'd much rather know now. I hate mysteries. But if it is anything against the old man . . ." he added, his voice rising heatedly, "I warn you . . ."

"Not now," interrupted Saint Hubert. "Leave it for tonight, *mon cher*. I was a fool to say what I did; I never meant to speak of it so soon.

"I would rather wait until you know your Father better. You must trust me to tell you when the right time comes. Until then, forget it, and forgive me for preaching."

Caryll's mumbled reply was inaudible, and in silence they walked on over the loose ground, each conscious of a new feeling of restraint that seemed to have risen between them, each wondering what was in the other's mind.

On entering the big tent Caryll was baffled as he looked at his Father's face. Within a few short hours he had seen its expression change from utmost ferocity to utmost gentleness.

He wondered with a feeling of perplexity what was the true nature of the Father of whom he knew so little, of whom he was to know more "when the right time came."

His eyes still lingered on his Father's face. And again he was puzzled by the unrecognised resemblance that had haunted him since the previous afternoon.

It was an elusive likeness that did not seem to be altogether complete, but which was sufficiently striking to make him rack his brains in a futile endeavour to remember where he had seen a similar face.

All signs of tears were gone from Diana's face as she entered; smiling and composed, she stood for a moment, a radiant vision in softest clinging white against the dark background of the black and silver curtains.

Then with a little gesture of mock contrition she came forward.

"I'm too late even to apologise," she said gaily, "so I shan't say any more about it. But I tremble to think what the soup will be like."

"Boiling, probably."

"Excellent, as it always is."

The Sheik and Saint Hubert spoke simultaneously, and as the former went to the door to clap his hands to summon the servants, the latter sat down beside his hostess and turned to her with his customary pleasant smile.

With a growing feeling of wonder, Caryll found himself becoming more and more interested in his surroundings.

Barbaric as were the appointments of the tent and bizarre though they seemed to him, he could not but admit that the costly furnishings were harmonious in their appearance and tasteful in their arrangements.

And, looking more attentively, he saw many little touches and devices that bore evidence of a woman's hand.

Strange home for an Englishwoman, and strange woman to find happiness and contentment in such an environment!

He glanced at her covertly. Then, sure that he was unobserved, he looked closer. Looked until there came to him the first faint stirrings of something he thought was merely admiration, but which changed swiftly into a deeper, warmer feeling that set his heart beating oddly.

How young she seemed, how absurdly young to be his Mother! He had pictured her so differently.

He had never imagined anything like the reality, had never imagined that she would be so beautiful. So beautiful and so sweet.

His Mother!

The term that before had been only a form of words became suddenly invested with new and wonderful meaning that brought an unexpected and wholly disconcerting lump into his throat.

Dinner was almost over. The silent-moving Arab servants had withdrawn, and only Gaston remained, serving the coffee that had been prepared over a brazier outside the tent.

There had come a pause in the conversation.

It was the Sheik's voice breaking the silence that roused Caryll from the reverie into which he had fallen.

"Do you go north or south when you leave us, Raoul, or are you going straight back to France?"

A moment or two elapsed before Saint Hubert answered. His gaze fixed dreamily on the plate in front of him, he went on arranging and rearranging a little pile of date-stones with the point of his silver fruit-knife.

"I am not going back to France," he said at last. "I am going to Morocco."

There was a curious deliberation in his reply, an almost sinister inflection in his voice that brought the Sheik's eyes quickly to his face.

"With any definite object?" he asked.

Saint Hubert looked up slowly and nodded. "With a very definite object," he said quietly. "I am going to find Réné de Chailles' murderer."

The little gasp that came from Diana was drowned in the Sheik's deep-toned exclamation.

"De Chailles' murderer!" he echoed incredulously. *"Bon Dieu!* I thought you had given up all hope of finding him. It is years since you have spoken of it, and ten years at least since the Government circulated a report that he was dead."

"I know," replied Saint Hubert, "but I was never quite satisfied in my own mind that that report of his death was correct. I got word from one of my agents that the man, or someone very nearly resembling him, had been seen in Morocco; he was a Moor, you will remember, though it was thought he was heading for the South again.

"It was a very slight clue, of course, but something definite at least, and I determined to follow it up. Curiously enough, within the same week I was approached in Paris by the legal representative of the De Chailles family.

"At the time of the tragedy, as you know, Ahmed, Réné de Chailles had a child, a baby girl about two years old. When he was murdered, the child and her Mother disappeared at the same time as the murderer.

"They have never been heard of since, and their fate is wrapped in mystery. But it has become necessary now to prove whether that child is alive or dead, for, by a series of rather startling deaths in the De Chailles family, this girl, if she is alive, has fallen heiress to considerable wealth and property.

"There are other claimants to the inheritance, distant relatives who are very naturally trying to make good their own claims.

"But the Courts refuse to move until they receive positive information that the elder branch of the family, as represented by Réné's daughter, has died out.

"So, at the moment the litigation rests in abeyance. Meanwhile, I continue my search with a twofold object: to hunt down the murderer of my poor friend, and to find his child, or prove her death."

There was a little pause when he stopped speaking.

It was Diana who spoke first, her smooth forehead wrinkled with perplexity.

"But when did this terrible thing happen? Why have I never heard of it before? You knew, Ahmed. Why didn't you tell me?"

The Sheik shrugged slightly, without looking up from the cigarette he was lighting.

"You could have done nothing, *ma mie*. Why sadden you unnecessarily?" he replied coolly.

Knowing him as she did, she guessed that something lay hidden behind the evasive answer, and her eyes lingered for a moment on his inscrutable face before she turned again to Saint Hubert.

"Who was *Monsieur* de Chailles and why was he murdered?"

Saint Hubert shook his head.

"If I could answer that last question it might have made my search easier, but the real reason for the crime has never transpired.

"Réné de Chailles was one of my oldest

friends. He was the youngest son of the Comte de Chailles, whose property adjoined our own in Dauphiné, and whose family is accounted one of the oldest in France.

"Always a visionary and a dreamer, he devoted his life to scientific research that gave him a world-wide reputation, though it did not bring him much material gain.

"Wedded to his work and painfully shy with women, we thought him a confirmed bachelor, but when he was about forty he fell in love with a very beautiful girl, some twenty years his junior, and married her.

"Despite the disparity in age, it was a marriage of affection on both sides, for she was as penniless as he, and as charming. She made light of his poverty, and she was thrilled with excitement at the thought of sharing his wild and roving life. The desert presented no terrors to her so long as she might be with him.

"I saw them when they started off on the long honeymoon that lasted until he was murdered, and I have rarely seen so ideally happy a couple.

"I saw them again the following year at Biskra, just after the birth of the little daughter whose coming made their happiness complete, and they were still wrapped up in each other.

"It was while visiting them there that I heard first of the new personal servant Réné had engaged to take the place of a devoted attendant who had recently died, after years of faithful service.

"Unfortunately, I never saw the man, for he had been sent south to organise the caravan for their forthcoming trip, or my subsequent search for him might not have lasted so long.

"Réné, enthusiast that he was, was loud in his praises. Impractical in many ways, and somewhat given to hasty likes and dislikes, my poor friend set very little value on references, and preferred in all matters to trust to his own judgement.

"I made my own protest, and made it pretty strongly, but Réné was infatuated with the fellow, and grew quite heated in his defence.

"He declared that in Ghabah, the Moor, he had at last found the ideal servant, and that he, Réné, was perfectly satisfied and preferred to trust to his own opinion.

"Of course, as he took up that attitude, there was nothing more to be done. They left Biskra as soon as *Madame* de Chailles was strong enough to travel.

"I never saw them again. But in the course of the next two years I had one or two letters from Réné, full of his love for his wife and child, who seemed to thrive marvellously in the desert, and full of hopes for the success of his expedition.

"And always he spoke in glowing terms of his paragon, Ghabah. Never had there been so devoted a servant, never had he received such intelligent assistance in the work that lay so near to his heart.

"The result of his blind confidence I heard from the lips of a dying camel-driver in the hospital at El-Oued. Knowing of my friendship with De Chailles, the authorities telegraphed to me in France as soon as they learned of the tragedy.

"I started off at once for El-Oued to glean what I could from the sole survivor of the party.

"The poor fellow was in a terrible state. He seemed to have determined not to die before revealing all he knew and satisfying himself that justice would be done. He gave his story on oath.

"It appears that Ghabah, while exercising a most extraordinary influence over De Chailles, was extremely unpopular with his fellow servants.

"Cruel and vindictive by nature, amongst other unpleasant attributes, he was credited with having the 'evil eye.' He seems to have deliberately set himself to win De Chailles' complete confidence.

"At the same time he was determined to detach from him his old followers, who might have interfered with his own schemes. His machinations appear to have succeeded without De Chailles having the least inkling of the plans that were to lead to his ultimate destruction.

"Overawed by the Moor, and fearful of his supposed evil powers, one by one the old followers fell away, and strangers took their places.

"The camel-driver himself had been with them only six months, but in that short time he had come to love De Chailles and his wife, and he worshipped the little girl, who, for some reason, had grown attached to him.

"Secure in his sinister reputation, the Moor remained unsuspected. But it was known that *Madame* De Chailles did not share her husband's sentiments; it was known that she too hated and feared him.

"And so great was his influence that even her remonstrances failed to shake De Chailles' faith, and he seems to have seen in his wife's distrust merely a woman's caprice, and to have treated it as such.

"The end came with cataclysmic suddenness. The entourage, not very large to start with, had, as the result of several recent dismissals, become smaller and smaller until only a handful remained

—two or three personal servants, and six or seven camel-drivers.

"On the night of the tragedy, the Moor, alleging negligence on the part of the men, collected all the rifles belonging to the camp and took them away to his own tent, on the pretext of overhauling them.

"Things had come to such a pass that no one dared to oppose him, and the men gave up their guns, unwillingly perhaps, but gave them.

"That night, the camel-driver who told me the story had a raging toothache, so he left the camp-fire round which the rest of the men were sitting, and went and lay down at the back of De Chailles' tent.

"There he always slept, and tried to sleep in the hope of forgetting his pain. But sleep would not come to him. And, placed as he was, he was in a position to hear and see all that followed.

"Later that evening the Moor came to the tent and held a long conference with his master. And after he was gone, the camel-driver, for the first time, heard sounds of dispute between De Chailles and his wife, who was sobbing bitterly.

"Then came silence, and the camel-driver said he thought he must have dozed for a little while. At any rate, there was an interval during which nothing happened.

"Then, all at once, he was awakened by the sound of a deep groan, and a smothered shriek sent him to his feet, sweating with terror. He seems to have hesitated for a few moments, too frightened to move and not knowing what to do.

"At last, love for his master and mistress conquered his fear, and slitting the canvas wall of the tent with his knife he forced his way into the room.

"I shall never forget the look on his face when he told me what he saw. De Chailles was lying on his back on the rug, stone-dead, with a knife thrust through his heart.

"*Madame* de Chailles, dead too, or having fainted, lay across her husband's body, her face hidden in his blood-soaked breast.

"The child, evidently just aroused from sleep, was crouched beside them, with her tiny hands twined in her mother's long dark hair, calling to them.

"Oddly enough, it was the sight of the child that spurred the camel-driver into activity. He rushed out of the tent, with only his knife as a weapon, to witness the final act of the drama that eventually cost him his own life.

"Too late to warn the others, for the Moor, a revolver in each hand, was before him. The light of the fire made the murderer's aim easy, and, a brilliant marksman, he shot them down, unarmed and defenceless as they were, like sheep.

"The horror of this ruthless massacre seems to have turned the camel-driver berserk. With no thought of his own peril, with no hope of escaping his comrades' fate, he sprang at the Moor, yelling like a madman, until he too fell, riddled with bullets.

"It was almost dawn when he recovered consciousness. All round him was death, and a silence that was terrifying.

"Bathed in blood and faint with exhaustion, he managed to hack some strips from the dead men's clothing and bandage what seemed to be the worst of his wounds, and then made his way painfully back to the tent.

"It was some time before he could summon

up sufficient courage to enter. Nerving himself at last, he struggled in. De Chailles still lay where he had fallen, his sightless eyes wide open and staring.

"But of *Madame* de Chailles and the child there was no sign. They had vanished in the night with the murderer. Gone too were the camels, as he discovered later, and with them certain of the more valuable equipments of the camp.

"As I have already told you, he was eventually picked up by a passing caravan and brought into El-Oued. He died happy that he had lived long enough to tell his tale, and rejoicing in the thought that his sworn vengeance was to be carried on, though he himself could not live to take part in it."

There was a moment of tense silence after Saint Hubert brought his tragic story to a close.

White to the lips, Diana sat rigid, her pale mouth set, her wide eyes misty with tears. Only the Sheik appeared to be unmoved, partly because he had heard the harrowing tale before, partly because he rarely allowed himself to give visible expression of his feelings.

But even his face was a shade sterner, and his deep voice deeper than usual, when at last he spoke.

"But the motive for the crime?" he said slowly. "De Chailles was too notoriously poor to be killed for his money—his possessions too few and too inconsiderable to make such a desperate venture worth the murderer's while.

"The Moor must have had some other, stronger desire than mere petty plunder. There seems to be only one possible solution left: he wanted the woman."

Saint Hubert's lips tightened.

"I suppose so. Such, at any rate, was the camel-driver's opinion. He had on one or two occasions seen Ghabah looking at *Madame* de Chailles rather peculiarly, but he had never dared to hint at such a thing even to his fellows. God grant that she died soon, poor thing."

"God grant it," murmured the Sheik. "He is sometimes more merciful than man."

And for once his iron will failed him, his usually even voice sounding curiously husky and constrained, while a look of unutterable sadness crept into the fierce dark eyes that were fixed on his wife's face.

"But if she should still be living, oh, Raoul ... if she should still be alive!" Diana exclaimed.

Saint Hubert made a sudden gesture of repulsion.

"I pray God she is not. I pray God that when He gives this man into my hands I may find with him only the child, the child who is *Comtesse* de Chailles," he added, with a queer break in his voice.

"But a woman now, surely, your *Comtesse* de Chailles?" suggested the Sheik, recovering himself with an effort. "Are you forgetting how many years it is since her Father was killed?"

Saint Hubert smiled half-sadly.

"A woman indeed, or nearly so. She must be about seventeen, if she is alive. I always forget that. I can only think of the baby I saw in Biskra."

"Poor baby ... poor Mother," whispered Diana. "It would have been far, far better if they had died then, while they were happy."

"A thousand times better," said Saint Hubert swiftly. "But who could have imagined then what was in store for them? Who could have guessed what the future held for that little dark-eyed baby?"

The Sheik turned to him suddenly, a rather curious look on his face.

"Suppose your search is rewarded, suppose you find this girl," he said with marked deliberation. "Do you still hope, considering what her life has probably been, to be *able* to take her back to France, to restore her to her inheritance?"

Saint Hubert shrugged rather hopelessly, and slowly shook his head.

"God knows," he answered, sighing. "I try not to think of that. Sufficient unto the day—I can only go on with my search, and pray that the All-Merciful Father has seen fit to protect her from—from what is almost inevitable."

Throughout the telling of the story, Caryll's eyes had never once left Saint Hubert's face. His fastidious mind revolting from the sordid horror of the desert tragedy, he was conscious of a vague feeling of shock.

Morally healthy, he had never cared to speculate on the primitive passions that move mankind to deeds of violence and shame.

Tonight he had had vividly brought before him lust in its cruellest form, and a crime which, though it sickened him, yet gave rise to thoughts that stirred his chivalrous instincts to their very depths.

His breath came quicker with the sudden heavy beating of his heart. Why did he think of Touggourt and the slender, sad-eyed Arab girl who had made so deep an impression on him?

Would the lost heiress for whom Saint Hubert was searching resemble her in any way? The sumptuous tent seemed to fade away, and he saw again the palm-shaded garden where once he had met her before the fateful evening that had swept her out of his life.

Dreaming, he forgot the present, forgot everything but the brief romance that had been so sweet, so fleeting.

"Salaam alikoum."

Caryll came down to earth with a start. The deep soft tones were his Father's, and at first he thought it was the Sheik who had spoken.

But his Mother's sudden cry as she sprang to her feet made him turn quickly in the direction of the door towards which she was flying with outstretched arms.

And with a little gasp he fell back in his chair, his face gone colourless, his hands clenching and unclenching as he stared once more at the tall Arab-clad figure and handsome, sinister face of the man he had seen in the Café Maure at Touggourt.

A blaze of anger went through him as his mind leaped to the truth.

So that was the resemblance that had made his Father's face seem so curiously familiar! Feature for feature they were alike.

It was only the absence of the great disfiguring scar on the forehead which, altering the younger man's expression, had made him fail to recognise what was so obvious to him now.

His brother! Good God, what a complication, and what an infamy!

Was it possible that the Mother who had flown so eagerly to meet him knew anything of the life of the son she was welcoming with such passionate demonstrations of joy?

If she knew what he, Caryll, had seen in Touggourt, would she not rather have shrunk from him with the same feelings of disgust and aversion that were his?

Blinded by his own furious indignation, he did not see the softening of the hard young face that was bent over Diana's, nor did he hear the tenderly whispered "little Mother, little Mother" that repaid her for the many weeks of anxiety and suspense.

And when at last the long embrace terminated, it was only with a deeper feeling of scorn and contempt that he watched the swaggering step and almost aggressive bearing of the younger Ahmed ben Hassan as he swept slowly across the room towards his Father.

Predisposed to condemn, he judged solely by outward appearances. It was not possible for him to know the inward trepidation and misgivings that were hidden under that assumption of bravado.

The Sheik had not moved or spoken since his younger son's sudden and somewhat dramatic entrance. Sitting where he did, he was in a position to see what the others had not noticed until the deep-voiced Arab greeting had drawn their attention to the presence he chose to ignore.

He uttered no word and made no sign, his mind apparently wholly engaged on the cigarette he was smoking.

And now, his black brows drawn together in a heavy scowl, he awaited the Boy's approach in the same silence.

Nor did he speak until his son, who had bent swiftly to touch his Father's shoulder with his lips, stood upright before him again, facing him with steady eyes in which defiance and appeal were curiously mingled.

And then the few low-spoken words of rapid

Arabic were audible only to the ears to which they were addressed.

The Boy made no reply when the Sheik stopped speaking, but his hand went mechanically up to his forehead in a salute that was as humble and deferential as any tribesman's, before he turned with a rather forced smile to greet Saint Hubert.

His enthusiastic welcome would have lasted longer had not Diana interposed between them with a laughing word of protest.

"Don't monopolise him altogether, Raoul. Spare him to Caryll for a minute. I want to see my sons shake hands."

But despite her happy face there was a quiver in her voice that betrayed the emotion she was endeavouring to conceal and tears were very near the surface as she watched the meeting to which she had so long looked forward.

And it was with emotion no less great than hers, but arising from very different causes, that Caryll found himself stumbling to his feet and stammering some kind of response to the easy greeting of his younger brother.

His brother—his rival!

Ashamed no longer of the love which, grown faint, now rushed back into his heart with almost overwhelming intensity, he longed to shout aloud the secret that so strangely united them, longed to beat the truth from those scornful smiling lips.

Since *he* was here, what of the hapless girl who had been his victim?

Quivering with jealousy and rage, Caryll forced himself to take the slim brown hand that was stretched out towards him.

Chapter Seven

Only Caryll saw that swift glance of menacing warning. To the others the meeting between the two brothers appeared perfectly normal.

But in spite of that, a feeling of constraint seemed to come suddenly over all the occupants of the room.

There was rather an awkward pause while they gathered again about the table, the Boy sitting close to Diana, whose eyes kept wandering anxiously to the great scar on his forehead, of which for the moment she would not allow herself to speak.

The relief of his presence was enormous.

But she was still troubled with the mystery of his long absence and beset with imaginative speculations as to the nature of this last escapade, from which he had returned bearing visible signs of having passed through some great danger.

And her trouble was augmented by the thought of the coming interview between Father and son that was inevitable. His disobedience could not go unreproved—that she allowed without hesitation—but what would his punishment be?

Furtively she glanced at her husband, but the Sheik's face was inscrutable.

He would be just, as he always was just, but if justice demanded, he would be merciless, even to his own son. His law was one and the same for son or tribesman.

After the meal was finished Saint Hubert and Caryll left, and the Sheik told the Boy to join him outside.

Both silent, they started to cross the open space that separated them from the main camp, the Boy's breath quickening with every step as he strove to rally his fast-oozing courage to meet the wrath that was to come.

Still in the same ominous silence the Sheik paced on past the army of low *guitones* that housed his followers; past the long lines of picketed horses; past the big herd of kneeling camels gurgling and grumbling as they chewed the cud.

At last he came to the spot where, until tonight, the Boy's double tent, a miniature copy of his own, had stood, with the two smaller ones used by Ramadan and S'rir near it.

But now the place they had occupied was empty, and looking for them the Sheik saw only two fidgeting horses held by an Arab, whose prompt salute did nothing to lessen the heavy scowl that was gathering on his Chief's face.

"What new whim is this?"

Flushing under his Father's stare, the Boy moved uneasily, his eyes wavering.

"I camp at El-Hassi," he muttered at last, with obvious reluctance, naming a tiny oasis that lay about five miles away to the south.

The Sheik jerked his head angrily.

"In the name of all devils—why?" he demanded.

The hot flush deepened in the Boy's face.

"I have reasons," he faltered in a voice that was scarcely audible, his tongue passing rapidly over his dry lips as he realised the inadequacy of his answer.

For a moment the Sheik glowered at him. Then, with a shrug of the shoulders, he called to the Arab who was holding the horses.

Guessing his intention, the Boy sprang forward, clutching at his arm.

"My Father, if you would listen to me here, or if you would wait until tomorrow..."

But with a quick gesture of refusal the Sheik shook himself free.

"I will listen when and where I choose," he retorted, and his tone made further remonstrance impossible.

The waiting Arab was S'rir, as patently ill-at-ease as his master, and with his heart grown heavy as lead, the Boy took the reins that were thrust into his unwilling hand when his attendant mounted and cantered back to the camp to execute the Sheik's order.

Leaning his head against the big stallion's satiny neck, the Boy waited for what seemed an interminable time, his thoughts ranging forward with miserable apprehension.

For what was coming he had only himself to blame. Bitterly he admitted it. By no reasoning could he justify what he had done.

He had broken his word; he had been absent without leave, and that in the face of the most stringent orders—sufficient reason alone for his Father's anger.

But he had more than that to answer for, more than that to face when the little camp at El-Hassi was reached.

And yet, what else could he have done?

His hands were wet as he struggled with the sudden impulse that came to him to make a clean breast now of everything, and throw himself on his Father's mercy, while there was still time.

Gripping his courage, he half-turned, looking back over his shoulder.

But the impulse had come too late. Already the horse and escort the Sheik had sent for were approaching, and, surrendering his own mount once more to S'rir, who had returned slightly in advance of the little troop, the Boy went slowly to hold his Father's stirrup.

It was Eblis that had been brought, in a fit mood to match the temper of the man who was to ride him, and employing some of Diana's gentle persuasion, the Sheik dragged the plunging animal to a standstill and, waving his son aside, leaped into the saddle.

Finally they reached the tiny oasis, watered by an underground river, that showed a few ragged thorn trees and scattered bushes of stunted scrub.

Close by the trees that clustered round the well from which the oasis derived its name lay the small encampment, the missing tents they had come to find, and with them the low striped shelters of the body-guard the Boy no longer disdained.

The little double tent was pitched apart from the others, and from its half-closed entrance-flap came the soft red glow of a lamp.

Moments seemed like hours to the Boy as he waited while his Father, still silent, held back his restless horse and sat motionless, scowling down on the peaceful scene beneath.

Racked with suspense, it was almost with a

feeling of relief that he saw the Sheik at last signal to the escort to remain where they were, and then ride slowly down the steep slope.

Together they reached the level and dismounted, turning their horses over to S'rir, who led them away to the distant camp-fire.

And, the actual moment come, quite suddenly the Boy's endurance snapped.

"My Father..."

Never had his voice sounded so humble, so full of entreaty. But the words that were trembling on his lips died away unspoken, for the Sheik turned to him swiftly, silencing him with upraised hand.

"Wait," he said tensely, and went towards the tent.

But as he neared the half-opened door he paused, and stood as if listening. And standing rigid beside him, the Boy also heard the sound that stayed him, and a spasm of pain convulsed his face.

How often in the last few weeks he had heard it before, that plaintive, crooning lullaby sung in the sweet, low, girlish voice which, tearing at his very heartstrings, made him sometimes almost forget the treachery that had turned love to hatred.

With a stifled utterance that might have been either a groan or a curse, the Sheik thrust aside the partly closed flap and swept into the tent.

Beside an inlaid stool where coffee-cups and cigarettes were placed, the singer was crouched, half-sitting, half-lying on a pile of cushions, her slender figure swaying to the rhythm of her song.

Absorbed, yet listening, her quick ears caught the rustle of the heavy burnous, and dropping the guitar she raised her head eagerly.

But the glad cry of welcome quavered and broke as she sprang to her feet, her slim hands clutching at her breast, her wide eyes, startled as a frightened fawn, wandering with a look of wondering amazement from one to the other of the two set faces so curiously alike, so curiously different in their expression.

For an instant she stood. Then, with another smothered little cry, she dragged the loosened veil across her face and, turning with a quick lithe movement, ran to the shelter of the inner room.

"Who is that girl?"

For the first time in his life the Sheik spoke to his desert-bred son in English, and before the cold fury of his face the Boy gave back a step, his own face blanching.

"It is a woman—I took," he returned shortly, flinging his head back with a sudden gesture of defiance.

The Sheik's eyes flashed dangerously.

"You—*took!*" he repeated trenchantly. "You can speak of it so easily?"

And then, like the breaking of a dam, the passionate temper that characterised him burst beyond control.

The anger that for the last hour had been accumulating within him boiled over and found vent in a torrent of words that, burning and pitiless, scorched the very soul of the son who stood white-lipped before him.

Quivering as each hard thrust struck home, the Boy waited in sullen silence while the storm rolled over his head. For some time after the Sheik ceased speaking, he said nothing.

Then, very slowly, he glanced up, looking at his Father strangely.

"You have cursed me for what I have done,"

he whispered, with shaking lips, "but how did you take the little Mother?"

The Sheik's face went suddenly as white as that of the Boy, and he flinched as if a bullet had touched him.

"You know that?" he said heavily.

And in a quick revulsion of feeling, unable to endure the look of torment that had leaped into the dark eyes fixed on him, the Boy turned away his head, his short-lived triumph gone, hating himself for the revenge that a moment ago had seemed so sweet.

"I have always known, since I was so high," he answered, very low, his hand reaching down to the level of his knee; "and Gaston nearly killed the man who told me."

The Sheik made no comment.

Sweeping his hand across his face, he flung back his burnous as if the weight of it oppressed him, and, moving to the door, he stood with his back turned to the room, looking unseeingly out into the night, wrestling with the bitterness and shame that filled him.

The repetition of his own sin!

The remembrance of his own misdoing brought home to him vividly in the person of his son, the son to whom he had transmitted the vicious strain that was in his blood.

It was his fault far more than the Boy's, for the taint was hereditary. And, knowing it, had he failed in the responsibilities that parenthood had laid upon him?

Too much the Chief, too little the Father, he had allowed more freedom than was advisable under the circumstances, trusted too much to the steady influence of time, not realising how acute had become the necessity for interference.

And now—this open liaison with a native girl!

With a heavy sigh he turned back to the room and, going to a divan, motioned the Boy nearer.

"Since you know so much," he said, and the words came from him draggingly, "it will make plain speaking easier between us. You have thought fit to remind me, and I admit your provocation, that what you have done I did before you.

"I cannot deny what is known to every man who was with me at the time, even if I wanted to, which I do not—though I have always prayed, for your Mother's sake, that you might never know the shame I put upon her. But you cannot shelter yourself behind my sin.

"You will have to pay, as I paid. You may argue that it is a common enough occurrence, that you are only sowing your wild oats, as the majority of men do—as I did myself.

"But am I to make no protest when I see my own son going the way I went? God pity you if you ever experience the same regret and self-loathing that has been my punishment for twenty years."

The scorn in his flashing eyes and the bitter contempt of his tone sent the colour rolling in a dark wave over the Boy's face.

"I ask your pardon," he burst out passionately, "and I am ready to take any punishment you may choose to impose on me.

"Nothing can make me feel less respect for myself than I do, nothing can be worse than the hell I have lived through these last weeks. But the girl..."

Despite himself, his eyes wandered to the curtain that divided the two rooms.

"... I have to keep."

There was a sudden huskiness in his voice that made the Sheik look at him narrowly.

"You love her?" he asked.

And in a flash of memory time slipped away, and he seemed to be listening to Raoul de Saint Hubert asking that same question twenty years before.

"*No!*"

But the very vehemence of the emphatic denial left the Sheik wondering.

"Then why did you not leave her?" he asked dryly.

The Boy's hands went out in a gesture of helplessness.

"With whom could I have left her?" he cried. "With Sliman, or any of his kind, to use as I have used her—for a day, a week, till the fancy passed, and then to throw away to greater shame than I have brought her to?

"Vile as I am, I am not so vile as that. For all the hateful life she led with the foul brute who owned her, she was unsoiled, clean and pure as her own name-flower, until I took her, and made her what she is. . . ."

His voice broke and for a moment he could not speak.

Then he went on hurriedly.

"But even if she were not what she is, I could not have let her go, for she has knowledge that I have not yet been able to get from her that is necessary to us, that is concerned with those matters of which I have to tell you."

His Father looked up quickly.

"Is this matter urgent?"

"Very urgent."

"Then you had better tell me now. The other

difficulty," the Sheik nodded towards the inner room, "can be settled later."

It was only a bald outline of facts the Boy rehearsed, but, fresh from his own experience, it was sufficient to give the Sheik food for thought that momentarily became more serious and pressing.

"Of course you saw Mercier in Touggourt, and told him of this?"

The Boy shuffled and looked away.

"No—I—there were difficulties," he stammered, flushing deeply.

For the incident of the Café Maure was a detail he had omitted from a narrative that had been full of blanks and only sketchy in outline.

Checking the natural question that sprang to his lips, the Sheik clicked his tongue against his teeth and jerked himself to his feet.

"Then a report will have to go to him at once," he said decisively. "A delay now might be fatal. You say you lost sight of this agreeable trio before you left Touggourt, but your description of them will be something more to go on than we have had so far.

"You will have to come back with me now, and we shall need Saint Hubert's help. He is *au fait* with the whole situation, insofar as Mercier could enlighten him."

But as he gathered his burnous round him, he glanced back over his shoulder and then at the Boy again.

"This girl," he said slowly; "you say she betrayed you to the men who mistook you for a secret-service agent, that you struck at them through her and kept her for the information she possesses.

"But that does not altogether explain the

position in which I find her here. Did you take her only as a revenge for the injury she did you and for the knowledge she holds, or was I right just now in supposing her to be your mistress?

"I want the truth, Boy. Is she or is she not what I take her to be? Was it a momentary impulse to which you gave way, and have since regretted, or have you been consistently living with her?"

For a second the Boy stood wavering.

Then with a scarcely audible word of assent, he flung away and, dropping down on the divan, buried his head in his hands.

"She has been with me for three months!" he said in muffled tones.

The Sheik swung round with a violent exclamation.

"Three months!" he echoed. "Without love as an excuse? Before God, Boy, I don't understand you."

But as he spoke a dark flush crept over his tanned cheek. Had love been *his* excuse so many years ago when he had himself taken a woman by force, not as revenge for any injury she had done him, but for mere lust and for hatred of the race she represented?

Driven by bitter memory, he started to pace the room, but after a couple of hasty turns he halted again beside the divan, his hand resting for a moment on the Boy's shoulder.

"Did you never think how this was going to end?" he said more gently than he had yet spoken. "Did you never think what might be the probable result to both you and her?"

"I don't know—I didn't think—I—*oh, God, if I'd never seen her!*"

The hopeless misery in the Boy's voice made

the Sheik wince, while it strengthened the unpleasant conviction that for some time had been steadily growing upon him.

Unwelcome as was the thought, he found himself unable wholly to believe the emphatic denial hurled at him earlier in the evening.

His firm lips closed in a straight hard line of determination. There was no use in dwelling on it.

No matter how deeply the Boy's feelings were involved, he could never consent to such a contravention to his principles.

"Too late to wish that," he commented gravely. "What is done cannot be undone. You will have to think of the future now, and think to some purpose. Obviously, in view of the information you say she possesses, she must stay here until we have got that information.

"After that, I shall have to see what arrangement can be made for her. But you must understand clearly, Boy, that this liaison has got to stop —*now*. You will give me your word?"

It was long before an answer came, so long that once or twice the Sheik glanced frowningly at the watch on his wrist and moved restlessly.

But with patience that was unusual to him he waited in silence.

Behind him, the Boy writhed on the divan, his face crushed against his hands, struggling with the conflicting emotion that warred within him, that had warred perpetually since the first night when he had taken her, making his life a hell that at times had been almost unendurable.

Shame and remorse strove with a still-unsatisfied longing for revenge. He had fulfilled his vow. He had made her pay as he had sworn she should pay, and still he wanted her.

Why? It was not love. Love killed by treachery and deceit could never live again. It was only hatred he felt for her now.

Then why was the promise demanded of him so difficult to utter?

Why did the thought of her stir him as it was stirring him at this moment?

It was not love but mere physical desire that stayed him, not love but desire that was quickening his pulses and driving the hot blood through his veins till he almost cried aloud with the agony of longing that swept over him.

He wanted her! Though the sight of her was torment, he wanted her!

To let her go, never to feel her trembling in his arms again, he could not. Yet what other course was open to him?

For all its quiet utterance, the request for his promise had been a command, a command that might not be disobeyed.

His Father's will was law, and refusal would not help him. It would only mean banishment to one of the distant camps and a humiliating curtailment of his liberty.

And the girl? What would it mean to her?

In the last few weeks a subtle change seemed to have come over her, and she had taken refuge in a dumb reserve that baffled his understanding.

She had ceased her passionate avowals of love, from which he had turned with disbelief and scorn.

That she wept often in secret he knew, but in his presence she was mute and dry-eyed, submissive and rebellious by turns, but silent even when she struggled against his embraces.

Yasmin, whom once he had loved! Yasmin, who had betrayed him!

With a choking sob he leaped to his feet, his set face almost grey under the deep tan.

"I will give you my word," he said, his voice hoarse and shaking uncontrollably, "but I can't tell her now, not tonight."

For a moment the Sheik looked fully and searchingly into the haggard dark eyes that were so like his own; then he smiled suddenly, a smile the Boy had never seen before, a smile that only Diana knew.

"Then tell her I need you," he said gently, relapsing into the more familiar Arabic, "but tell her quickly. And remember, I trust you!"

And swinging on his heel, he went out of the tent.

The Boy's face was very bitter as he divided the communicating curtains and passed slowly through into the inner room. She took no notice of his coming.

Sitting motionless on the rug, she did not even lift her head at his approach. But he knew that she was conscious of his presence, for as he drew nearer he saw her tremble, saw the tiny hands clasped round her updrawn knees clench convulsively till the knuckles shone white through the soft brown skin.

His heart beat with sudden violence as he looked at her, his eyes ranging hungrily over her slim young beauty till his mouth grew parched, his body taut with the hold he was putting upon himself.

Outside in the moonlight his Father was waiting, but moment succeeded moment and still he stood silent, unable to tear his gaze away, unable to frame the words his dry lips refused to utter.

At last, with an effort, he forced himself to speak.

"There is work elsewhere for me tonight. You are not afraid to be alone? You are safe here with Ramadan and S'rir, and the others."

It was not what he meant to say, nor had he ever before shown consideration for her, or given the least indication that he was sensible of any womanly weakness she night be supposed to possess.

But tonight the sight of the drooping little figure huddled at his feet was compelling him, despite himself, to a sense of pity he had never thought to feel again.

Yet why should he pity her, he asked himself bitterly, when his absence could only mean relief from the tyranny of a master she feared.

Still, there was no expression of relief, no visible emotion of any kind in the dark unfathomable eyes that met his only for a moment.

"Of what should I be afraid?" she countered quietly.

But there was something in her tone that sent the blood rushing into his face, that moved him to sudden and inexplicable anger.

"Of what, indeed?" he retorted, with sharp sarcasm, "since *I* will not be with you."

Her face hidden against her knees, he could not see the trembling of the delicate lip she caught between her little white teeth, or the quick rush of tears that wet her cheek.

And when she spoke, it was not in answer to his taunt.

"Who was the man who came with you just now?"

Surprised at the question, he scowled down at

her suspiciously. Was she still trying to solve the secret of his identity, which had never yet been revealed to her, still hoping by some circuitous means to aid the men from whom he had taken her?

"He is the Sheik, Ahmed ben Hassan," he said shortly.

Then with a mocking smile:

"The demon who rides swifter than the tempest and whose eyes blast like the fiery bolt from heaven. The demon who cannot die—my Father."

She shuddered violently. But as if impelled by something stronger than her fear, she raised her head swiftly, looking at him with strange intentness.

"Is it he who needs you? Is it only to him you go?"

There was a note of almost fierce anxiety in her voice, but, spoken very low, only the first part of her question reached him.

He nodded, pulling his burnous closer and moving a step nearer.

"It is not only me he needs and what I have come to bring him," he said significantly. "He needs also the knowledge you have, the knowledge you will not give me. Is it not better to tell me now than to wait until he forces you to speak?"

It was a direct threat that made her shudder again, but still her fearful eyes looked steadily into his.

"How can I speak of what I do not know?" she said wearily. "I have told you again and again that I know nothing."

He jerked his head with angry impatience, his passionate temper flaming at what he thought was obstinacy.

"You have told me many lies," he returned harshly, "but here you will find that lies will not serve you."

And with a short, hard laugh he flung towards the door.

"*Lord!*"

But the wailing cry of entreaty did not stop him, and, leaping to her feet, she fled after him, clutching at his arm.

He did not mean to strike her, but in turning to thrust her from him, his hand struck heavily against her heaving bosom, and with a little piteous moan she staggered back, catching for support at the draperies that fell to behind him.

For a moment she stood with closed eyes, trembling from head to foot. Then, her hands pressed tightly over her aching breast, she slipped through the curtains and ran quickly to the door.

Screened by the half-shut entrance-flap, she watched him mount and join the other horseman, whose very name filled her with superstitious terror and dread.

She watched them ride side by side up the steep slope till they reached the summit, where the waiting escort, drawing aside to let them pass, closed in behind them, hiding them from view.

He had gone!

Shivering, she turned and looked at the empty room. This evening, when she had been brought here after the long hard journey that had been like a terrible dream, after the nights passed lying at his side, aching with weariness, under the open sky, it had seemed like a haven of refuge.

And now . . .

Blinded by the tears that suddenly rained down her face, she stumbled back into the inner room and dropped to her knees by the bed, burying her head in the soft mattress, gripping at the silken coverlet with wide-flung hands, writhing in the desolation of loneliness that overwhelmed her.

He had gone, and gone in anger and disbelief. Would he never believe, never turn to her again, he who had loved her once, who had compelled in her a love that not all his harshness and brutality could kill?

He had left her, he who was the light of her eyes, her world, her very existence, and would he ever come again?

Though he did not love her anymore, he had needed her, and with even that she had been content. But now, did he not even need her?

Here, amongst his own people, was there not perhaps some other whom he loved, some other with a better right than hers to whom he had gone?

Was this the end, tiring of possession, his passion of vengeance satisfied? Was she now only a useless encumbrance, to be flung aside, unwanted, unremembered?

Never to see him, never to hear his voice, never to feel his strong compelling arms? How could she live without him, her life, her Lord!

Prone on the rug, rent with great sobs that seemed to shake her slender frame to pieces, she wept in a very abandonment of grief, whispering his name until, exhausted, she lay still, facing the truth that seemed inevitable.

He would never come again. She was nothing to him now. He had gone ... and with him had gone everything.

Everything? Her burning face pressed closer into the thick rug that was damp with her tears. Not everything.

One thing she had that could not be taken

from her. In her loneliness and misery, one hope, one joy, remained.

A hope she had never dared to tell him, a hope that was to be her secret strength and consolation until the living comfort came to fill her empty arms, and to lie on the breast he had bruised with his angry hand.

She had longed for death, but how could she die when under her heart lay the precious gift that had been his only mercy?

His child . . . to love and live for.

A cry of anguish burst from her. The child alone could not satisfy her starving heart.

It was the Father of the child she wanted, the Father of the child for whom she was aching and longing, whose name she murmured with a passionate yearning.

Terrible sobs racked her while the long slow hours dragged wearily past, till one by one the guttering candles flickered and died, and she lay in the blackness, alone with her despair.

Chapter Eight

It was still very early in the morning when Caryll woke from the brief sleep that had lasted barely a couple of hours.

The rest of the night had been spent in tossing restlessly from side to side of the narrow camp bed, and in pacing the tent until the need of fresh air and further space had driven him out into the moonlight, to tramp up and down in a fever of inward tumult.

Was it love indeed he felt, or only jealousy? An insensate jealousy he had never thought to know, which brought with it a cold and furious rage that made him fearful of his own thoughts and of the passion of hatred that was seething within him.

In that first moment of recognition, when he had realised the identity of the man he had last seen in the Café Maure at Touggourt, he had seemed to see him through a haze of red.

It had been all he could do to keep back the denunciation that sprang to his lips, to take the proffered hand and make some rational reply to the courteous greeting that had been so contradictory to the menace in the other's flashing eyes.

The girl was an Arab. She could never be anything to him. Then why did the thought of her disturb him so deeply?

He flung over onto his side with a groan, crushing his hot face into the crumpled pillows as he forced himself at last to meet the plain truth.

Was physical desire love? Did he want her now, as he had never wanted her before, only because of the strange jealousy that had come so suddenly upon him—the mere animal jealousy of the thwarted male craving revenge?

In heaven's name why should he be jealous? In no sense had she ever been his, whereas the other...

Was there nothing but torment in this accursed country? That horrible story Uncle Raoul had told last night—and now this!

Scarcely had he drunk his tea when Williams reappeared, stepping diffidently, and in obvious embarrassment.

"Beg pardon, m'Lord," he hesitated, "but the young gentleman what came in last night..."

He paused as if searching for a suitable title; then:

"Your Lordship's brother, m'Lord," he stammered finally.

With every nerve in his body gone taut and rigid, Caryll looked up slowly, and jerked his head enquiringly towards the door.

"Yes, m'Lord," replied Williams in answer to the unspoken question.

For a moment Caryll sat silent, his heart beating furiously.

"Ask him to come in," he said at last, and his cracked, harsh voice sounded in his ears like the voice of a stranger.

He did not move when the tall, picturesquely

clad figure swept into the tent, and his eyes were coldly hostile as he marked again the arrogant bearing and faintly insolent expression that had roused his antagonism last night.

It was the Boy, moving forward with nonchalant self-assurance, who spoke first.

"I offer my profound apologies for so early an intrusion, *Monsieur*," he began in French, "but your man told me you were awake, and I may find no other opportunity today of speaking with you alone."

"Can't you speak English?" Caryll demanded sharply, as his brother sat down.

The Boy waved his hand airily, his white teeth flashing in an amused smile that only served to exasperate Caryll more.

"I can—if I must," he replied in the same language as before, "but I prefer to speak French."

Caryll scowled at him angrily.

"Well, what is it you want at such an early hour?"

The bland manner and careless smile were gone when the Boy turned to answer his question.

"There is, I fancy, some small need of explanation between us, and I am here for that purpose."

He paused for a moment, looking searchingly at the hostile face on the other side of the table.

"Last night was not our first meeting," he went on more slowly. "We met before at Touggourt. And I have come to you this morning to suggest that it would be more—shall I say politic —if you were to forget an incident which, after all, can have no personal interest for you."

A note of irony crept into his tone.

"It was unfortunate that you should have witnessed it. But, since you did, may I hint that it would be—er—more unfortunate if you were to refer to it before others whom it does not concern. Do I need to be more explicit?"

Again Caryll saw in his eyes the gleam of menace he had seen last night, and he sprang to his feet, quivering with passion.

"Damn you, no!" he cried furiously. "You've said enough, and more than enough. If I choose to hold my tongue about that affair at Touggourt, it won't be any consideration for you that will keep me silent.

"What you are pleased to do, insofar as it affects yourself, doesn't concern me in any way—you can go to the devil in your own fashion as quickly as you like, for all I care.

"But what touches the honour of our family does concern me. It's enough that I saw that terrible business; I'm not likely to be in any hurry to let the whole world know that my brother is a blackguardly seducer. Need I be any more explicit?"

The Boy leaped to his feet, and for a moment they stood facing each other, both livid and shaking with uncontrollable fury.

The atmosphere of the little tent seemed suddenly to have become charged with electricity, alive with naked human passions, while the flashing dark eyes stared down fiercely into the steady blue ones that stared as fiercely and as resolutely in return.

Then, with a tremendous effort, the Boy recovered the self-command that had almost slipped from him.

His clenched hands unclosing, he stepped back a pace.

"Thank you, I understand perfectly," he said suavely, though a faintly mocking smile curved his set lips. "Your confidence and your candour make any further explanation between us unnecessary.

"And as I cannot pretend to imagine that my company can be either pleasing or welcome to you, I hasten to relieve you of it as speedily as possible."

He had reached the open door when a muffled "Wait" arrested him, and he halted, not troubling to look round, his hand resting lightly on the rolled-back canvas entrance-flap.

"*Monsieur?*"

"Where is she?"

The sudden question quickened the burning jealousy that was still smouldering, and, suspicious and resentful, he turned swiftly.

"What is that to you?" he snarled.

Then, all at once, his face became expressionless, his eyes narrowing until the long dark lashes almost hid them, and he shrugged with pretended indifference.

"Since you ask," he said smoothly, "she is in my tent—at El-Hassi."

And he jerked his hand carelessly towards the south.

Hardly able to control himself, Caryll came a step nearer, staring passionately.

"What are you going to do with her?"

The Boy laughed bitterly.

"What am I going to do with her?" he repeated slowly. "*Mon Dieu,* I know no more than you. If you had asked me what I have done to her I should have told you that that was my business, and not yours, *Monsieur mon frère.*

"But when you ask me what I am going to do with her, you have come to the wrong person for the information you want. Because I was fool enough to bring her here, she has passed from under my control.

"Have you not yet been long enough in the camp of Ahmed ben Hassan to learn that here only his will and pleasure matter? Ask *Monseigneur,* if you want any further news of the girl."

Caryll went white to the lips.

"What do you mean? My God, what do you mean?" he whispered shakily.

For a moment the Boy scowled at him perplexedly, then he laughed again, a soft little laugh that was full of contemptuous scorn.

"Not what you evidently mean," he said acidly. "Even our Arab morals are not so bad as that. And *Monseigneur* would hardly thank you for suggesting that he keep a harem."

And with another scornful laugh he swung on his heel and strode out of the tent.

"She is in my tent—at El-Hassi."

Again Caryll heard the smooth, even voice, again he saw the mocking smile that had accompanied the words, and he swept his hand across his face, struggling against the jealous rage that still filled him, striving to forget both his brother and the girl.

He was relieved to find that only his Mother was lunching with him, and as soon as he finished the meal he hurried back to his own tent again.

Through a blur of tears Diana watched him go, then, alone once more, she went wearily to the divan, to wrestle again with the fear that had never left her since last night.

What had happened after Father and son had gone out together into the night, leaving her to intolerable apprehension that had kept her awake almost until the dawn?

Hour after hour she had waited in misery for

the Sheik's return, and hour after hour had passed and he had not come. At last, from sheer exhaustion, she had fallen asleep.

But sometime during the night he must have returned, for, waking long past her usual time, she saw by the rug and pillow left lying on the divan that he had been and gone again.

She tried to be grateful for the consideration that had made him refrain from disturbing her, but suspense was worse to bear than anything he might have to tell.

And all day he had been absent. All day she had seen nothing of the Boy. That he was in Saint Hubert's tent she knew from Gaston, but Gaston had also intimated that they had both been up all night, and were now sleeping.

So she had forced herself to wait, striving to put from her the recurring "Why? Why?" to which she could find no answer.

Poor, lovable, headstrong Boy, what had he done this time that kept him even from the Mother who never reproached and always forgave, no matter how great the offence?

She was standing beside the little bookcase, mechanically turning the leaves of a book she knew by heart, when the Sheik joined her.

Vaguely comforted by just his mere physical strength, she gave way for a moment, lying speechless in his arms.

And realising her need, he held her closely, silent himself, until at last she looked up, her tear-wet eyes entreating.

"Ahmed, tell me ... surely I've waited long enough! I know why you let me sleep—it was good of you—but I would rather you had wakened me.

"What is wrong with the Boy that he won't

come to me? I don't know anything. I haven't seen anyone since last night, except Caryll, who only came in for lunch and went away directly afterwards, and he was so...so strange, and looked so upset.

"Oh, what does it all mean? I must know. I can't bear this mystery any longer."

And looking down on her quivering face, the Sheik knew that in trying to spare her he had only made her suffer more, and he swore at himself softly under his breath.

"I don't know what is wrong with Caryll," he began, "but the Boy..."

He paused, and though she did not shrink from him, swift fear leaped into her eyes.

"Ahmed, what have you done to him?"

His arms tightened round her.

"Nothing! His going at all was, of course, inexcusable. But that he stayed away so long as he did was not altogether his fault."

And he proceeded to tell her what he knew.

"That isn't everything, Ahmed," she said slowly; "there's something behind all this, something you are keeping back. I can see it in your face. I saw it in the Boy's face last night. What has he *done,* that he won't come near me?"

But even though he knew that sooner or later she must inevitably come to learn of it, still he tried to keep from her the knowledge that would only give her pain.

Crushing her to him, he bent his tall head and kissed her with passionate tenderness.

"Let it go, *ma mie,*" he said huskily. "The Boy's been a fool, but it's over and done with. Raking it up again won't mend matters. He's been playing with fire for some time, and he's burnt his fingers at last.

"And this time his folly has brought its own punishment, a punishment that hurts more and will last longer, I believe, than anything I could do to him."

But the trouble only deepened in her eyes.

"I can't let it go. I must know. What has he done?" she cried, and the sharp anxiety in her voice made him wince.

Still he hesitated. And with a great sob she pulled his head down, staring at him almost fiercely.

"I'm his Mother ... I've the right to know ... he's my son as well as yours, Ahmed," she said, panting.

He thought of her half-laughing, half-serious words the night before, and looked away with a heavy sigh.

"Not yours, this one, *ma mie*," he said bitterly; "mine, in every respect, God help us both."

And very gently he told her, omitting nothing.

Long before he was finished, her face was hidden against the dark cloth of his burnous, and from time to time he could feel the faint shudders that ran through her as she listened to him in silence.

All her sorrowful mother-love, and all her distress and disappointment, were expressed in the cry that broke from her:

"Oh, Ahmed, how could he?"

The Sheik's dark eyes flickered, and a look of pain swept across his face.

"*Grand Dieu!* You can ask me that, remembering what I did to you?" he cried, more bitterly than before. "He did it because he is my son, because the desire for women has been the curse of our family for generations.

"You know what my Father was until my Mother's disappearance cured that and his other failing; you know what I was until you came into my life.

"The Boy has only conformed to type, and I can't blame him as much as I blame myself.

"And I've failed you as well as him, and the fault is mine more than his. You've got me to thank for this sorrow, my wife, not him. He . . ."

But her soft hand was over his mouth, silencing him.

"You've never failed me," she interrupted passionately, "never once in all the years we've been together. You've helped me always in everything.

"And even this . . . this trouble isn't so hard to bear when we can share it. We're one, Ahmed, even in this. And if you have failed him, then so have I failed him, for I've always thought of the possibility, I've always feared.

"But he seemed so young still, I never remembered how the years were slipping away. I never realised he was a man . . . until last night. And then, his face . . . Oh, Ahmed, my Boy . . . my Boy!"

She broke down, sobbing bitterly. And he carried her to the divan, holding her till she grew calm again.

It was long before she lifted her head to look not at him but at the strong brown hands she held between her own.

"And she is with him . . . now . . . at El-Hassi?" she whispered with a little shiver.

The Sheik moved restlessly.

"At El-Hassi, yes. With him, no. I told you it was over and done with," he said, rather shortly.

But still she sat motionless, battling with the sudden mother-jealousy that was tearing her heart, that forced from her at last the almost inaudible question.

"What is... she... like?"

Smothering something she could not hear, the Sheik got up abruptly, moving to a table in search of a cigarette.

"Pretty, of course," he shrugged, "or the Boy would never have looked at her. And yet 'pretty' is hardly the word. She is rather beautiful, undeniably so.

"In every way an uncommon type, and I don't know how to place her. She is said to be a Moor, but I doubt it. She is very quiet and shy, and most curiously refined-looking for a dancing-girl. Altogether she baffles me."

"Does she care for him?"

The Sheik scowled at the glowing end of his cigarette.

"I'm afraid so," he admitted reluctantly.

"And he?"

"God knows, I don't. He swears he hates her, and I think he's lying. But whether he does or does not makes no difference.

"I would have sent her to one of the other camps last night if it had been possible, but unfortunately she has information regarding the men she has been associated with, which she refuses to give. Until she speaks, she will have to remain at El-Hassi.

"I saw her again this morning, and though I tried every means, short of personal violence, to induce her to tell me what she knows, she refused to say a word that would give any clue to these people or their activities.

"She was obviously sick with fear the whole

time, and seemed obsessed with the idea that we were all devils, or, at any rate, something supernatural and unpleasant. The old myth of the Ben Hassan, I suppose.

"Her obstinacy was exasperating, but I couldn't help admiring her courage; even her own personal fear was not able to shake her loyalty. And she's only a child, a slender slip of a thing, with eyes like a frightened gazelle.

"But she has the spirit of a regiment. Heaven knows how she comes by it. I don't often own myself beaten, but I've only once before in my life been so completely defied, and that was also by a woman."

He laughed softly as his eyes turned with a very tender light in them towards the woman in question.

It was only a fleeting smile she gave in response, and then her head drooped again, and she sat, silent, struggling with the impulse that every moment was growing stronger within her.

Suddenly she seemed to make up her mind, for she rose and went to him, her pale face flushing with the effort she was making.

"Ahmed, I would like to see her."

For a moment he stared at her in astonishment, the smile dying from his lips.

Then his mouth set in the hard, straight line she knew so well.

"It's out of the question, Diana. I absolutely refuse."

And his tone was such that it took all her love and courage to persist.

"But, Ahmed..."

He made as if to turn away, his black brows knitting.

"*Ma mie,* I have said it is out of the question. That he should have brought her here at all was insult enough to you, but that you should see her, *bon Dieu*, no, it's impossible!" he added vehemently.

But though she paled she stood firmly, her fingers twined in the folds of his burnous to stay him, her eyes looking straight into his.

"You don't understand," she said hurriedly; "you can't, you're only a man. But I'm a woman, and it's all different to me. I can't leave it like that.

"I've got to do something.... Oh, Ahmed, don't you know what I mean? We're responsible, you and I, as well as the Boy. It's horrible... but if she is only a child, as you say she is, and if the Boy... if... if anything... has..." She faltered, and the colour rushed back into her face.

"There isn't anything," broke in the Sheik quickly, unclasping her clinging hands. "I thought of that, too, and I asked the Boy this morning."

She shot him a look of gentle scorn.

"As if he would know! She would never tell him."

He shrugged impatiently.

"As to that, I can't say," he returned with a touch of irritation. "But even if it were so, which heaven forbid, it does not alter the case, or my decision. You will leave El-Hassi alone, *ma mie*, and trust me to make proper provision for the girl, whatever happens.

"And don't torture that tender heart of yours by imagining the worst when there may be no necessity for it."

And as if to put an end to the discussion, he went to the writing-table and sat down to read over the dispatch that was waiting for the evening courier.

But it was only a pretext, as Diana very well knew, for, without the further information that seemed destined to remain unspoken, there was nothing to add to the report the Sheik and Saint Hubert had evolved during the early hours of the morning.

Unsatisfied, she went slowly to the divan again, and sat with her eyes fixed on her husband's uncompromisingly turned back, still endeavouring to find a way to what her conscience urged her.

He had smoked one cigarette, and was lighting a second, when her voice reached him, a softly tentative voice that was little more than a murmur.

"Suppose that girl won't say what you want her to say ... won't you let me go to her, then? She might speak ... for me."

With a violent oath he flung down the match and swung round in his chair.

"Diana," he cried angrily.

Then he laughed, the black scowl smoothing from his face as he eyed her, half-amused, half-affectionately.

"You perfect woman. I might have guessed you would try and get round me in some way. But I have already told you I do not wish you to see her. Don't make me put it plainer.

"The girl will speak, sometime. As a matter of fact I am pinning my hopes on Raoul.

"As you know, he has a very persuasive tongue, when he likes. And he may be able to convince the superstitious young person that he is not a djinn or an afreet, as she seems to think I am, but an ordinary mortal like herself, and so gain her confidence.

"Anyhow, it is worth trying. He is at El-Hassi now, may Allah prosper his eloquence," he added in Arabic, with a faint smile that was not very confident.

He had hardly spoken when Saint Hubert came in.

The look on his face sent both the Sheik and Diana to their feet and across the room to meet him, the former with cool composure that was habitual, the latter with a wildly beating heart, fearing she knew not what.

Dropping into a chair the Sheik pushed forward, Saint Hubert sat for a few moments, breathing heavily.

And it was not until he heard the piteous break in Diana's imploring voice that he looked up, shaking his head slowly.

"No, no, nothing fresh has happened," he said, speaking with an effort. "Forgive me for frightening you. It's only that I've had a—a shock, and I'm a bit—upset."

He turned suddenly to the Sheik, his haggard eyes dark with pain.

"I have been to El-Hassi, Ahmed, to see the girl..." he went on, jerkily. "And I saw instead a ghost, the ghost of a woman I saw sixteen years ago in Biskra, and I think I have found De Chailles' daughter.

"It was Isabeau de Chailles' face and eyes, Isabeau de Chailles' voice that spoke to me, Isabeau de Chailles as I saw her one night, dressed as an Arab woman to please her husband."

His shaking voice trailed into a whisper, and he covered his face with his hands to shut out the look of horror that had leaped into Diana's eyes.

And in the silence that ensued he heard behind him the cracking of the frail top bar of the chair on which he was sitting as it splintered like matchwood under the sudden pressure of the

Sheik's hand; heard, too, Diana's groan that was like a cry of torment.

"Réné de Chailles' daughter, in my son's tent, oh, my God!"

Saint Hubert sprang up, forgetting his own distress in the suffering he knew must be greater than his.

"Mon ami..."

But, already master of himself again, the Sheik flung round to confront him, his feelings hidden behind the mask-like expression that made his face so often inscrutable.

"You'll have to prove that, Raoul," he said, almost violently, as if struggling against something he would not allow himself to believe.

"It is only resemblance and a supposition you are working on. I shall want more than that before I can accept this—this idea, of yours, before I can do anything to—to..."

He broke off, biting his lip; his scowling gaze travelled from Saint Hubert to the dearly loved wife, whose unhappiness hurt him far more than his own.

He went to her slowly.

"You'd better go and lie down, Diana," he said, his hard voice changing to indescribable tenderness.

"You've had about as much as you can stand. It won't help you to hear what Raoul has to say, and we shall have to try and clear up this miserable business, somehow, as soon as possible."

She lifted a white face of entreaty.

"Please, please, Ahmed, don't send me away," she whispered tremulously, "let me stay."

Unable at that moment to refuse her anything, he nodded assent, lingering for a moment to settle the cushions of the divan more comfortably round her. He put his lips to her bright hair before he turned again to Saint Hubert.

"Now, Raoul."

Saint Hubert dragged a chair nearer.

"First, the information you want," he said rather wearily.

"I'm sorry, Ahmed, but I haven't got it. While admitting that she hates and fears this Moor for the cruelty he has always shown her, that she hates and fears his stranger companions for reasons she will not disclose, she refuses to give any information concerning their doings in Algeria.

"She knows nothing, but finally I made her talk of her life.

"A sad little life, how sad and wretched I don't think she properly understands—spent wandering continually all over the Barbary States, but mainly in Tunis, though last year they were in Morocco, where almost most of her earliest recollections seem to be.

"Last year in Morocco, you will observe, Ahmed, and it was last year that the Moor was seen there."

He stopped for a moment, looking keenly at the Sheik, and after a slight pause Saint Hubert took up again the thread of his story.

"I tried to get from her what were her earliest remembrances, but beyond the fact that the Moor was consistently cruel, her childhood recollections seem to be dim and shadowy.

"When I pressed her and tried to stimulate her memory, she spoke rather vaguely of a time when she was not alone with her brutal master, of some scarcely remembered person who was kind to her, who touched her with gentle hands instead of beating her, and who had a sweet voice and sang to her.

"Of one of these songs she seems to remember somewhat, just odd fragments, but though the tune is slightly reminiscent of an old French *berceuse,* the words were such a hopeless jumble of Arabic and French that I could make nothing of them.

"And she does not even know whether this dream-like person was a man or a woman. Mother she says she never had—I don't know what she thinks she has evolved from.

"I tried her with the name Ghabah, but it seemed to convey nothing; she gave no sign of knowing it, and I was watching her closely.

"So I have not really discovered anything that can be called clear proof of her identity, but for all that, I am absolutely convinced that she is the girl I am looking for. Her likeness to Isabeau de Chailles is too striking to be ignored.

"Until I can find this Moor, and prove definitely whether or not he is the same who murdered my poor friend, I hold this girl to be Isabeau de Chailles—she was named after her Mother."

"And if you prove your case?" The Sheik's voice was still hard and unconvinced, but Saint Hubert, who knew him, realised the struggle that was taking place behind that seemingly inexorable front.

"Let me prove it first, *mon cher,*" he said gently. "I may never find this man who alone knows the secret of her origin. And if I do find him," he shrugged expressively, "who knows what the outcome will be?

"In the meanwhile, I can only go on waiting and hoping. Thank God one can always hope!

But remember, Ahmed," he rose as he spoke, "that while I quite understand that for the moment you are more immediately concerned with this girl than I, her future—be she Isabeau de Chailles, or only some nameless waif of the desert—is my affair."

For an instant he stood with his hand resting on the Sheik's broad shoulder, then moved nearer to the divan, drawn irresistibly in spite of himself.

And the slim, cold fingers he stooped to kiss closed tightly about his own.

"Raoul, does she care, really, for the Boy?"

The broken whisper nearly unmanned him, and his face was very white as he looked down into the lovely, sorrowful eyes; looked with uncontrollable heart-hunger and longing at all the slender grace and beauty he had once held unconscious in his arms.

And his thoughts turned to another little slender figure who, barely an hour ago, had knelt at his feet in an agony of tears, sobbing for news of "her Lord who had gone from her in anger."

His lips quivered, and he shook his head.

"What do I know of a woman's heart?" he said, with more sad bitterness in his voice than Diana had ever heard, and passed out of the tent into the gathering dusk.

* * *

The three or four days that followed Raoul de Saint Hubert's startling announcement were difficult ones for all in Ahmed ben Hassan's camp.

Saint Hubert himself, who daily spent several hours with the lonely girl at El-Hassi, patiently endeavouring to pierce the cloud that seemed to lie over her childish recollections, returned from each visit more than ever convinced that in Yasmin he had found the lost heiress for whom he was searching.

Diana, predisposed, for many reasons, to believe him, still failed to move the Sheik's inflexible decision.

Still sceptical himself, or wishing to appear so, he listened in silence to all Saint Hubert's confident statements, and strenuously opposed Diana's pleadings.

That she should not go to El-Hassi he was determined.

And more than that, for some reason he would not explain, he refused categorically to allow to reach the Boy any hint of the girl's possible origin.

And in this Diana found herself obliged to agree with him, for the Boy's attitude made it impossible to foresee what effect the knowledge would have upon him.

Literally obeying his Father's order, he had never gone back to El-Hassi, leaving the girl to think what she would. And since the night of his return he had not only declined to speak of her, he had retired into sullen isolation, holding himself rigidly apart from the family circle.

Even Diana had only seen him once, a brief interview lasting barely five minutes, which had been painful and unsatisfactory to both.

A batch of young horses that required schooling had given him an excuse to absent himself, and his days had been spent arduously amongst the rough-ridden with whom he had toiled from sunrise to sunset, exhausting himself by hard physical exercise in a futile endeavour to forget.

Caryll had become almost as much of a recluse as his brother. Coldly reserved and as unapproachable as he had been at first, his appearances were brief and not more frequent than absolute courtesy obliged.

To Saint Hubert only he unbent somewhat, but even with him he was silent and constrained.

He had never mentioned the Boy's early-morning visit to his tent, had never again referred to the raid on the Café Maure, of which the Sheik still knew nothing.

Saint Hubert had guessed from the first, however, that the missing girl who had aroused Caryll's interest was one and the same with the girl who was now at El-Hassi.

The day after the Boy's arrival he had bluntly broached the subject of the raid, and had asked Caryll a direct question concerning her abductor.

The query had been met with only a surly "Couldn't say. Shouldn't know the damn beast if I saw him again," but Saint Hubert had read the truth in his flushed face and the glint of anger that flashed into his eyes.

Hoping always for fresh light on the subject which almost entirely occupied his mind, he had told him quite frankly of his discovery that afternoon at El-Hassi, and, demanding confidence for confidence, had overborne his objections and drawn from him little by little all that he knew of the girl.

But Caryll had been able to add nothing to what Saint Hubert had already gleaned, and his first confidence had also been his last. Since then Saint Hubert had seen as little of him as had the others.

In this way, four days of tension had dragged slowly by, days of acute anxiety for Diana that only the Sheik's additional tenderness had made bearable.

But in one thing only he still opposed her, in one thing only he was adamant.

Even in his most tender, most yielding moments he still remained constant in his fixed determination with regard to the girl at El-Hassi, and not all Diana's entreaties could move him to alter his decision.

To El-Hassi she should not go, with his consent.

Dare she go without it?

During the last four days the thought had come to her often. Had she the courage to oppose him now?

Long, long ago she had learned obedience through fear, and the love that had come had made it easy. But for all her love, she knew, deep down in her heart, that the old fear still lingered.

Had she the moral strength to disobey him deliberately and face his inevitable anger?

He would never understand the reasons that were prompting her.

And it was the morning of the fifth day before Diana finally made up her mind that, in this one thing, she must be swayed by her own inner convictions . . . that, no matter what were the consequences, she must do what she firmly believed to be right.

Early that morning she had made her last appeal, and the Sheik's refusal had been even more curt and final than before.

All through the morning she had wrestled with herself, and it was nearly lunchtime before that decision was reached.

Because she believed it to be her duty, she would go to El-Hassi, and this evening, when

Ahmed returned, she would tell him what she had done.

If only she could have gone with his consent! But it was no good thinking of that. He would never consent. So she must go as she had planned, and go today, when his absence gave her the opportunity.

He had left, taking Caryll with him, for one of the distant camps that lay in the opposite direction from El-Hassi, and was not expected back until the evening.

It was only after she had watched them ride away that her courage almost went. But the thought of the girl kept her firm to her purpose, the girl who might be Isabeau de Chailles.

Her lips quivered, and for a moment she stood with her face hidden in her hands.

Then with a whispered "Oh, Boy, Boy!" she went through to the inner room to change into her riding-clothes.

Lunch was waiting when she returned, and a few minutes afterwards Saint Hubert came in, looking contritely at his watch.

"Late as usual. I'm sorry, Diana," he apologised, hurrying forward.

But as he reached her he paused, glancing at the table where only two places were laid.

"I didn't know you were alone," he went on, slipping into the chair beside her. "You shouldn't have waited for me. Ahmed told me last night he was going down to Ras-Djebel today, but where is Caryll? I thought he was here. His tent was empty when I looked in just now."

Diana helped herself to an omelette before answering.

"Caryll? Oh, he's gone with Ahmed," she

said at last, casually, as if the event were an everyday occurrence.

Saint Hubert's eyes widened with surprise but he checked the exclamation that rose to his lips.

"I'm glad," he said quickly. "It will give them a chance to—to become better acquainted. They have not had much opportunity so far. I have been wondering when our poor old hermit was going to come out of his shell."

Diana looked up with a rather odd little smile.

"He didn't come. He was pulled."

"You mean that it was Ahmed's suggestion?"

"Suggestion? My dear Raoul, when does Ahmed ever suggest? I heard the message he sent through Gaston this morning, and by the wildest stretch of imagination it could hardly have been called a suggestion. Caryll went to Ras-Djebel because Ahmed left him no option."

"Still, even so, it was a move in the right direction."

Diana shook her head slowly.

"I wonder. I have even been wondering if, perhaps, it would not have been better if Caryll had never come at all.

"He seems to have no wish that we should become better acquainted. I have tried by every possible means to make him feel that he is welcome and at home, but he gives me no encouragement."

She rose abruptly from the table, turning away to hide the tears that she could no longer conceal.

"It is the fault of circumstance, I think," Saint Hubert said slowly.

"The fault of circumstance," he repeated, as

she looked at him uncomprehendingly, "and there have been—complications since he came that have made these last four days very difficult for us all."

"But how can those complications affect Caryll? He is totally unconcerned with our affairs, his brother's included. He has never once spoken of the Boy, or wondered why he lives as he does.

"He is as indifferent to him as he is to us. And oh, Raoul, I prayed so hard that my sons might be friends."

And Saint Hubert, who knew what she did not, could only shrug hopelessly.

"It's early days yet, and it's all very strange for him. Give him time, Diana, and don't give up hope. Perhaps when this present difficulty is cleared away..."

Saint Hubert's voice faltered, and Diana took him up swiftly.

"If it ever is!" she cried despondently. "Oh, Raoul, what is going to be the end of all this trouble?"

Saint Hubert shrugged more hopelessly than before.

"God knows," he answered shortly.

And for a time there was silence between them.

Curled up amongst the cushions of the big divan, Diana lay staring into space, wondering how she could approach the subject that was in her mind; wondering whether Raoul also would oppose the thing she planned.

She turned to him impulsively.

"I wonder if any two people ever had so good a friend as you have been to us, Raoul," she burst out.

"You know what you are to Ahmed, but I

don't think you have the least idea of how much you have helped me ever since I've known you.

"And I can't begin to tell you . . . you'll just have to take it on trust, and believe that I am grateful."

"And have I nothing to be grateful for?" he answered, in a curiously muffled voice. "Has it never occurred to you to think what your friendship—and Ahmed's—must mean to a lonely man like myself?"

She laughed softly, shaking her head in protest.

"Nonsense, Raoul! Don't be so modest. You have more friends than you know."

But already her thoughts were veering, and her eyes grew serious again.

"You went earlier than usual to El-Hassi this morning, didn't you? Ahmed asked for you before he left, but Gaston said you were already gone.

"No, I don't think it was anything very important," she went on, in response to his look of enquiry; "only something about the Northern guards, I believe. He has called them in at last.

"I don't quite know why he wanted you to know. He was in a hurry, and he wasn't very explicit. Whatever it may be in other parts of the country, there has been no trouble anywhere near us.

"It was only because I was alone that they were sent out at all. With Ahmed at home, there isn't the least necessity for them, and he has been meaning to recall them for weeks."

She paused for a moment, her frank eyes veiled suddenly by the thick dark lashes that swept downward to her cheeks, her fingers twining and intertwining in evident embarrassment.

And when she spoke again there was note of hesitation in her voice.

"Have you found out... anything more... at El-Hassi, Raoul?"

"Nothing more, Diana."

"But you are still sure, still convinced...?"

"Still sure, still absolutely convinced," replied Saint Hubert quickly, "and if I can never prove it, I shall still be sure that I am right."

Forcing herself to composure, Diana rose to her feet and went to him, laying her hand on his shoulder.

"You wouldn't answer me when I asked you before, but tell me the truth now, Raoul, I beg of you. Does she really care for the Boy?"

Trembling under her touch, Saint Hubert looked up into her sad, questioning eyes. Looking only for an instant, he too rose, his face as white and strained as hers.

"Does she care?" he said huskily. "If you could see her, you would not ask me that question, Diana."

"I am going to see her... this afternoon."

At the unexpected reply he swung round with a sudden exclamation.

"No, no, it's impossible. Utterly impossible. Ahmed..."

"I know, I know," she broke in wearily. "Ahmed will be furious. But I can't help it. I've got to go. Even if she isn't Isabeau de Chailles, it makes no difference. She's a girl, in trouble and alone, with only men about her..."

"Not only men," interrupted Saint Hubert. "Ahmed sent a woman to be with her the morning after they came. Didn't he tell you?"

"No, he never told me that," she said slowly.

And for a moment she stood staring fixedly

at Saint Hubert, seeing not him but the husband she loved, the husband whose complex nature still held depths which even she had never yet fathomed.

She dragged her wandering mind back to the present with an impatient little jerk of the head.

"It isn't easy for me to go against Ahmed, but in this one thing I must judge for myself. I am going to El-Hassi... *now*. If you will come with me, I shall be glad. But if you would rather not..."

The reproach in his eyes checked her, and she gripped his hand contritely.

"Tell them to get your horse. I've got to go before I think too much about it," she said, with a shaky little laugh.

And as she moved away towards the inner room, she added over her shoulder:

"If you bring Mohamed we needn't take anyone else."

But there was no laughter in her eyes when she came out from the tent a few minutes later, and the extraordinary pallor of her face made Saint Hubert look at her anxiously as he watched her mount.

At last when they reached the high dune that overlooked El-Hassi Diana drew rein, looking down for a few minutes in silence on the little cup-like oasis beneath.

The wide brim of her helmet hid her face, but, watching her intently, Saint Hubert could see the nervous twitching of her fingers on the bridle that lay slack on her horse's neck, could see the rapid pulsing of her delicate throat where it showed above the open collar of her white silk shirt.

Then, still without speaking, she wheeled her horse to face the descent.

The camp had an almost deserted look, and only half a dozen men came hurrying with Ramadan to meet them.

And Ramadan, concealing what surprise he may have felt at Diana's unexpected appearance, salaaming with his usual gravity, hastened to apologise for the small guard that had turned out to greet her.

Mechanically returning his salute, Diana cut short his regretfully uttered excuses with a brusqueness that was foreign to her.

Signing to him to remove the horses, she went towards the little double tent.

But her step grew slower and slower as she neared it, and before the half-closed entrance she came to a sudden stop, shaking with nervousness.

Her agitation was such that Saint Hubert put out a detaining hand.

"Let me go first, Diana, to prepare her," he said gently.

But, shaking her head, she motioned him aside.

"I don't want her prepared; I want to see her as she is. Please wait . . . wait till I call," she said jerkily.

And, understanding, he let her go, stepping back as she passed through into cool dimness.

One swift glance showed that the outer room was empty, showed her, too, a scrupulous orderliness of arrangement that brought her a curious feeling of relief.

But it was not an empty room she had come to see, and she moved across the thick rugs, pausing for an instant beside the divan to fling aside her heavy helmet and push the thick, damp hair from her throbbing temples.

As she hesitated, shrinking sensitively from the interview she dreaded, there came from the inner room the sound of a sweet, low voice crooning softly.

Noiselessly she parted the silken curtains and stood looking, looking until tears of pity welling up in her eyes blurred her sight, at the graceful little figure that sat huddled on the floor in the middle of the room.

Unconscious of everything but her own unhappiness, the girl sang on, swaying slowly to and fro, her cheek pressed closely against something that lay half across her updrawn knees, half cradled in her arms.

Only a man's gaily embroidered jacket, a jacket Diana had seen many times before and recognised with a stab of intolerable pain and compassion.

And the girl herself ... a mere child, as they had told her, a slender, dainty, fragile-looking child, pathetically forlorn, and beautiful beyond her imagination.

But it was more than just her beauty that made Diana scan her delicately cut features with almost feverish intensity. It was a rush of intuitive feeling, inexplicable but overpowering, a sudden conviction that Saint Hubert had made no mistake.

Instinct, more strong than reason, clamoured within her that if Isabeau de Chailles lived, it was Isabeau de Chailles who sat before her now.

Isabeau de Chailles ... and the Boy.

Her weight sagged against the curtain she still held, and for a second she closed her eyes, suffering horribly.

But the momentary weakness passed, and she pulled herself together, racking her brains for some means whereby she might arrive at the truth.

How to prove it? How to succeed where Raoul had failed? Passionately she prayed for inspiration, and the thought that came rose from the depths of her own mother-love.

Perhaps Raoul had already tried it, but would not her woman's voice convey more than his deeper masculine utterance?

Softly, with infinite sweet tenderness, she breathed the name that might stimulate remembrance.

"Isabeau..."

"Maman!"

The wild cry echoed through the tent as the girl started to her feet, her face quivering, her wide-dilated eyes filled with eager, expectant joy.

"Maman!" she cried again, looking through and past Diana as though she did not see her.

"Maman!" she wailed again, like a terrified child. "Why did you never come? I heard you scream, and only *he* came... his hands all red and wet... and beat me...."

But the last words trailed into a faint, uncertain whisper, and she shrank back, shivering, her hands going gropingly to her head, the joy in her face changing to a look of blank bewilderment as the past receded once more into oblivion, and the partially opened door of memory shut down again inexorably.

Like a dreamer awakened from sleep, she sighed and murmured to herself, looking furtively about her as though searching for the vision that had vanished.

Then, for the first time, she seemed to see that she was not alone, and with a little gasp of astonishment she retreated farther, gazing with shy wonder at the slender figure that stood with outstretched hands and pitiful, shining eyes.

Again Diana called to her, but this time the name which had been so potent before aroused no answering chord in the girl's brain. Slowly she shook her head.

"There is no one here but me, and I am Yasmin," she said simply.

But already shyness was giving way to natural girlish curiosity.

And as she looked, half-timidly, half-questioningly, at the sweet-faced, strangely attired visitor who had broken in so unexpectedly on her solitude, she became vaguely conscious of a feeling stirring within her that gave her a sensation of trust and confidence she had never felt before.

Trembling with emotion she did not understand, she gazed back into the sorrowful, pitying eyes that seemed to be reaching down to her very heart, drawing her irresistibly.

Yielding almost unconsciously to their fascination, she came nearer, a faint smile curving her parted lips.

"In the name of Allah . . ." she murmured shyly, and pointed to a heap of cushions that lay piled in the centre of the room.

Grateful for the momentary respite, for she was totally nonplussed, Diana went to the little makeshift divan. For a time she sat silent, her hands straying over the silken pillows while she searched fruitlessly for words.

"Sit with me," she said gently.

And after a moment's hesitation the girl complied.

But still words would not come, and hunting for some pretext that might aid her to speech,

Diana's questioning eyes fell at last on the jacket that lay near her feet.

Stooping, she lifted it onto her lap.

"It's a coat of coats," she said admiringly, smoothing the creases from the crumpled piece of finery. "Surely it must belong to some great Sidi?"

Softly entreating, the girl drew it from her and held it jealously.

"It is my Lord's," she said falteringly, a wave of burning colour pouring over her sensitive little face.

"And what is the name of your Lord?" asked Diana, with lips that trembled uncontrollably.

But, edging away as though suddenly distrustful, the girl made an odd little gesture of refusal.

"He is just my Lord, I may not say his name," she whispered tremulously.

A great sob burst from Diana, and she grasped the slim, brown, twitching fingers tightly in her own.

"O child, are you so loyal to him, who has used you so badly?"

With a sharp cry the girl sprang to her feet, wrenching her hands free.

"Who are you?" she gasped. "What do you know of my Lord?"

Then, as no answer came, swift agony leaped into her tragic eyes, and she flung herself down in a passion of tears, clinging to Diana's knees.

"Why do you not answer me?" She sobbed. "What harm has befallen him that you will not speak? Allah, Allah, was it for this I dreamed of him last night . . . and of that other, who sought to kill him?

"In my dreams I saw them both struggling, both covered with blood . . . and then he fell . . . my Lord . . . a great knife in his chest."

Shuddering and moaning, she drew back, glancing up fearfully, her voice sinking to an awe-struck whisper.

"Are you a spirit? Is it because he is *dead* that you are here?"

With tears running down her own face, and unable any longer to resist the rush of tenderness that surged through her, Diana caught the trembling little sob-shaken body into her arms.

"No, no," she murmured huskily, "no harm has come to him. And I am no spirit, but a woman as you are ... who loves him as you do. Yasmin, Yasmin, can you not guess who I am? Did he never speak to you of me, his ..."

She broke off suddenly at a sound that sent her flying to her feet, her hand groping mechanically for the revolver she had not carried for years.

Almost unable to believe her own ears, she stood listening to the wild uproar that came from outside the tent, a crashing rattle of musketry and a hoarse shouting of hostile voices that carried her back to the time of dreadful memory, the time of Ibraheim Omair.

And, paralysed for a moment, she stared blankly into the face of the girl, who was gazing back at her with startled eyes in which a great fear was dawning.

Then, above the horrible din, came the sound of Saint Hubert's voice, shouting; and, roused into activity, she gripped the girl's wrist and hurried her into the outer room.

And as they ran there was a ripping of cloth behind them and the whining scream of a bullet as it tore its way through the costly hangings of the tent.

Ducking instinctively, Diana fled for the door, dragging Yasmin with her, and out into the open, to where Saint Hubert was standing, revolver in hand, still calling to her.

His face was the colour of ashes, and as she joined him he muttered something she could not hear, and his arm closed convulsively round her.

Clinging to him breathlessly, she looked for the cause of the tumult, and stiffened suddenly with a little gasp, while her heart seemed to miss a beat.

Towards them Ramadan and Mohamed were racing with the horses while round the body-guards' tents raged pandemonium.

Smoke from the rifles and swirling clouds of sand and dust made sight difficult, but straining her eyes Diana could see the tiny handful of her own people, who were gallantly endeavouring to hold in check six times their number.

Raiders . . . in Ahmed's territory!

The thought was almost incredible. And her own people . . . must she stand here and see them massacred before her eyes?

She turned to Saint Hubert with a sharp cry.

"Raoul . . . *the men!*"

"Never mind the men," he answered brusquely.

"It's you and the girl I'm thinking of. My God, why did Ahmed call in the Northern guard! Listen, Diana," he added hoarsely, his arm tightening unconsciously about her:

"If they reach us in time, Ramadan and Mohamed, get away as quick as you can. Don't wait for me or them, and ride as you never rode in your life. Thank God the horses are fresh."

Neither agreeing nor refusing, Diana only gripped his hand. At the same moment a deep groan burst from him and he thrust her back violently, interposing himself between her and what he did not want her to see.

But she had seen, and straining against his opposing arm, she stood unheedful of the hail of bullets that spattered viciously round her, staring at the oncoming raiders with eyes that had grown hard and glittering with anger.

Her own men were down, blotted out from sight as they were ridden ruthlessly underfoot. Only Ramadan and Mohamed were left.

And as she looked, Mohamed suddenly flung up his arms and fell sprawling onto the sand. And, crouching low in the saddle, three led horses beside him, Ramadan galloped alone.

With a roar of exultation, the raiders swept on, over Mohamed's prostrate body, nearer and nearer, till the noise grew deafening; till, with a terrible shudder, Diana saw Ramadan surrounded; till a piercing scream made her turn with swift apprehension to the girl who until now had stood silent beside her.

It was no stray bullet that had touched her but only terror that convulsed her face, that made her cower on the ground with her head buried in her arms, while she shrieked again and again the name that was on Diana's own lips.

One last spurt, another crashing volley of rifle-shots which, aimed high with evident intention, passed harmlessly over their heads, and the raiders were on them.

Turning suddenly, Saint Hubert flung the two women back against the side of the tent, and, covering them with his own body, he faced their assailants, shooting coolly and economically, but with a deadly fear in his heart that was not for himself.

For a minute only, then a hell of tumult broke out and of what happened during the next few moments Diana never had any very clear remembrance.

Deafened by the infernal noise, unable to see what was happening, a strange feeling of unreality came to her, a nightmare feeling that held her immobile, that left her with only one clear thought, the almost frantic girl whose screams she tried to muffle against her breast.

She had drawn her closer when, all at once, the wall of the tent against which she crouched seemed to give suddenly, and as the whole structure slowly collapsed, she felt Yasmin torn from her clinging arms, saw all round her a sea of strange faces and the trampling feet of horses.

And at the same moment Saint Hubert lurched and staggered back, and she went down on her face, crushed under his weight.

Prone on the sand, she lay gasping for breath, sick and dizzy with the fear that rushed back over her. But above her own fear came the thought of Raoul—Raoul, who had perhaps died to shield her.

Slowly and painfully she dragged herself out from under him and sat up, clearing her eyes and mouth of sand, wondering at the deep silence that had supervened.

Shivering from head to foot and huddling close to Saint Hubert's senseless body, she forced herself to look, shuddering, at the fallen bodies which lay strewn on the trampled, blood-stained sand, and saw that the majority of the surviving raiders were already in flight, heading for the north.

She raised her head and looked on the corpse-strewn plain, and she saw that she was not quite alone, for a figure had struggled up from amongst a tumbled heap of bodies and was coming slowly towards her.

With a feeling of unutterable relief she recognized Ramadan and ran to meet him.

Torn and dishevelled, and rocking unsteadily on his feet, with blood dripping from a deep gash on his cheek and his right arm hanging uselessly at his side, he seemed to hold himself upright only by sheer force of will.

Reassuring himself first of her safety, he went with her to Saint Hubert, and together they bent over him.

With a great contusion on his forehead, as though from a glancing bullet, and shot low in the body, he was still breathing.

But Diana read in Ramadan's troubled face a reflection of her own fear, and bitter tears filled her eyes as she gazed down on the death-like features of the man who was far dearer to her than her own brother, who had been the staunchest, truest friend a woman had ever had.

Would he die before help reached them? Was there nothing she could do to alleviate his suffering if he regained consciousness? Helplessly she glanced at the wrecked tent behind her, and then looked despairingly at Ramadan.

"Water!" she gasped. "Oh, Ramadan, can you reach the well?"

With a faint smile he drew himself straighter. "*Inch* Allah?"

But as he turned away stiffly, he paused beside the huge sprawling figure of the Moor who had been knocked down in the fight, and, looking closer, gave a sudden start and rolled the body over unceremoniously with his foot.

And staring down on the evil, blood-streaked face, he cursed as Diana had never heard an Arab curse before. Then, stooping, he made a hurried examination.

"Stunned," he announced laconically, and stood scowling in evident indecision, his left hand groping inside his burnous for the revolver he had recovered.

But before Diana could even guess his intention he shook his head and thrust the weapon back with a little grunt of regret.

"He was better in hell," he remarked coolly, "but I must not kill him, for my Lord will want this devil alive."

And, briefly explaining what he knew of the Moor, he callously withdrew the great knife from the other man's lifeless body, and hacked some pieces of rope from the broken cordage of the ruined tent.

But, with one arm useless, he was unable alone to carry out his purpose, and Diana's assistance was required before the prostrate giant was bound securely.

That done, he set out limpingly toward the well.

For a few moments Diana watched his halting progress, then with a heavy sigh she went to Saint Hubert and, sitting down beside him, lifted his head and shoulders gently onto her knees.

Reaction was setting in, and, dazed and stupid with shock, she still felt that she must be in the midst of some horrible dream, for the truth seemed too preposterous, too ghastly, to be real.

The thought of Yasmin nearly drove her frantic. In that short, strange interview her heart had gone out unreservedly to the girl who was suffering what she herself had suffered.

The common bond as well as the common love between them had awakened more than ordinary compassion, and when she had first taken her into her arms it had seemed almost as if God had given her the daughter she had always longed for, and never had.

And she might have been her daughter if ...

She caught her trembling lip in her teeth, forcing back the tears to which she dared not give way. Even if the Boy cared, even if love came to him as it had come to Ahmed, would they ever find her again?

So nearly accomplished, was this to be the end of Raoul's devoted search?

Raoul! She looked at him fearfully. Was this her fault? she wondered miserably. And if he died, would Ahmed ever forgive her?

He was stirring now in her arms, groaning and muttering incoherently, and Diana looked up with an impatient sigh, dashing the tears from her eyes so that she might follow Ramadan's dragging and laborious footsteps.

He had stopped by one of the fallen bodies, and she saw him bend down for a moment before moving slowly on again. Then, from among the distant tents, she saw another limping figure emerge, and soon the two men met.

Only two left, with Raoul, perhaps, dying ... and it might be hours yet before the remainder of the body-guard came in from the main camp.

Eagerly she grasped at the thought that perhaps some might have escaped the raiders and, bolting riderless for home, have already raised the alarm.

But the faint hope was taken from her when Ramadan returned with the other survivor, who was carrying a goat-skin of water over his shoulder.

Bruised and battered, but less damaged than Ramadan, the man came forward and knelt shyly beside Diana, tipping the goat-skin to enable her to damp her handkerchief and moisten Saint Hubert's lips.

Ridden down and left insensible early in the struggle, he had little to tell, and, not recovering until the raiders were in flight, he could only say that the horses had been taken as well as the girl, whom he had seen lying across the saddle of one who appeared to be the leader of the party.

But he recovered himself quickly and, with more confidence of manner than he had yet shown, announced that he was ready to go for help.

Diana looked at him uncertainly.

But it was a course evidently agreed upon between the men as they had walked back from the well, for Ramadan cut short her objections with the curt intimation that there was no other alternative.

If either of the two had to go, she preferred that Ramadan should remain, for she dreaded the Moor's return to consciousness, bound though he was.

The Moor was apparently also in Ramadan's mind, for before the young man set out, he called for his assistance in dragging the trussed figure farther from where Diana sat.

And not until that was done, and the messenger was well on his way, did he himself sink down, exhausted, on the sand, to watch his prisoner and regret for the hundredth time that he had not killed him when he had had the chance in Touggourt.

As she watched the long grey shadows stealing across the little cup-like oasis, a dread of the approaching darkness came to Diana, and she felt her mental grip weakening.

Endurance, stretched to the utmost, snapped suddenly, and in a terror of loneliness she stared panic-stricken at the tumbled bodies of the dead.

At Ramadan, collapsed at last and lying prone on the trampled sand; at Saint Hubert, remote and senseless in her arms; and crushed her hand against her mouth to smother the cry that burst from her.

"*Ahmed, Ahmed, come to me!*"

And even as she cried, he came. For an instant she saw him, struggling with his almost frenzied horse, silhouetted alone against the skyline.

Then, like a great white-crested wave rolling shorewards, his followers surged up over the ridge of the high sand dune and poured after him as he drove Eblis down the steep slope with reckless speed that sent Diana's hands flying to her throat.

Behind him in that mad rush Caryll and the Boy raced neck and neck, and near them she seemed to see Gaston and S'rir.

But her eyes were fixed on the big black stallion, on the dark, handsome face that was the dearest to her in all the world.

And before either sons of tribesmen could drag their maddened horses to a stand he had flung himself out of the saddle and reached her.

The next moment she was clinging to him, sobbing hysterically and imploring his forgiveness even while she gasped out the details of the raid.

But there was only love in his look, only love in the gentle pressure of his arms as he drew her away to make place for Gaston, who was already on his knees beside Saint Hubert.

"*Ma mie, ma mie,*" he whispered unsteadily, "since you are safe..." and broke off with a shudder that all his stoicism could not suppress.

Then with a tender word he laid her down and went to Saint Hubert.

The group of anxious-faced Arabs collected about the wounded man drew aside at his coming, and before they closed in round him again Diana had a glimpse of Gaston and Caryll, with up-rolled shirt-sleeves, and of something else that banished the faint tinge of colour that had begun to creep into her lips.

And when, a few minutes later, the Sheik came back to her and she struggled up to meet him, he saw rather than heard the question she could scarcely utter.

"Not yet," he said, with a forced calm, "but it's only a question of time. A few hours, perhaps a day or two. He's still unconscious, thank God. If we can only get him back to camp..."

He shrugged rather hopelessly, turning away to hide the emotion he endeavoured to conceal even from her.

It was what she had known in her heart from the first, and now the actual confirmation of her fear seemed to rob her of all power of speech and movement.

Through a haze of tears she saw Caryll push his way out from the group of men round Saint Hubert and join his Father.

She watched them as they went together to where the Boy was bending over Ramadan, who, supported against S'rir's knee, was talking rapidly, pointing at the now-sullen and impassive Moor.

It was the sight of the Boy that made her remember what, in her distress for Raoul, for the moment she had forgotten.

He had swung round to confront the Sheik,

his hands outstretched, as though in urgent supplication.

Too far away to hear she was, but near enough to see his lips moving in what seemed to her a desperate appeal, to see the look of terrible despair that lay in his eyes, to see, too, the heavy scowl that was darkening her husband's face.

Was Ahmed going to refuse? How could he, when he knew!

The girl's screams were still ringing in Diana's ears as she fled across the intervening space and thrust herself between them.

"Ahmed . . . Ahmed, for God's sake . . . for my sake, let the Boy go. She is Isabeau de Chailles. *I know it.*"

For a moment the Sheik stared down into her wet, beseeching eyes, then he looked at the Boy and nodded.

"Go with God," he said curtly, and shouted an order that sent half a hundred men into their saddles, yelling like maniacs.

But the tumult subsided quickly as they fell into orderly ranks. And in the comparative silence that ensued, Diana felt the Boy's arms close round her in a quick, passionate embrace, and heard his huskily murmured: "Little Mother, little Mother," before he tore himself away, with his Father walking beside him, to the horse S'rir had just brought up.

In honour, and in common humanity, he must go, and it was not for his Mother to try to keep him back.

The Boy's foot was already in the stirrup when a touch on his arm arrested him, and, turning, he looked into a face that was scarcely less strained and haggard than his own.

For an instant the brothers' eyes met and held.

Then with a gesture that was unmistakable, Caryll thrust out his hand.

"This is your job, not mine," he said hoarsely, "but if you'll take me with you, I'll be grateful."

Chapter Nine

In the big outer room of the Sheik's pavilion, Raoul de Saint Hubert was fighting for what little life was left to him.

Determined to live until the Boy returned, or until there should be no longer any hope of his return, with the girl who represented so much to them both, he seemed to be keeping death at bay by mere force of will.

The journey from El-Hassi had been a slow and anxious one, for the heavy ground made it difficult going for the bearers who carried the improvised stretchers that held the wounded man.

For Diana those five miles had seemed like fifty. Torn with anxiety for her sons, and fearing that each moment would bring the news of Saint Hubert's death, she had lain in her husband's arms, for he had refused to let her ride, shaking with reaction and tortured with fears.

Night had fallen when they got into camp. Worn out in mind and body, she had fallen asleep from pure exhaustion as the Sheik carried her to her bedroom.

She did not wake even when he removed her

long boots and stripped the blood-soaked riding-clothes from her weary body.

All through the night she had slept while the Sheik and Gaston watched in the adjoining room.

But strength had come back with the morning, and during the day she had taken her turn beside Saint Hubert, attending to his needs with the ready smile that always brought an answering flicker into his sunken eyes.

All day long the ordinary routine of the camp had been suspended.

A day of suspense that had seemed never-ending, that had racked Diana's nerves to the utmost, that had begun to tell even on the Sheik.

Early in the afternoon, yielding to his wife's entreaties, though himself refusing to admit the necessity, he had sent reinforcements to follow the trail from El-Hassi.

With them also went a band of specially mounted scouts to be posted at intervals along the route, that the news which was so anxiously awaited might be received with as little delay as possible.

Hiding his own anxiety, again and again he tried to allay Diana's fears, reminding her of the long start that had given the raiders several hours' advantage.

Reminding her, too, that unless they also had reinforcements, a contingency which he declared was almost unthinkable, the Boy's party considerably outnumbered the one they were pursuing.

But though she had listened to him patiently, though she had tried to find consolation in his arguments, he had seen her agitation become hour by hour more visible.

He had seen her face hour by hour grow

whiter and her eyes turning with a strained, hunted look in them towards the looped-back flap of the half-open entrance.

Lost in painful thoughts of the past, it was with a start that the Sheik realised that the wounded man's eyes were open and looking, with the ghost of the old whimsical smile, into his.

It was the old half-bantering, half-affectionate voice that spoke:

"Where were you, Ahmed?"

The Sheik shrugged slightly as he stooped forward to take the limp white fingers stretched out to him.

"In Hell, I think," he said rather bitterly, "or as near it, probably, as I shall ever get. The reality can't be much worse than the one we make for ourselves."

It was many years since the subject had been referred to by either, but Saint Hubert had always known the deep remorse that had tinged his friend's happiness, and tonight he guessed the train of thought that had provoked that bitter utterance.

He made a little gesture of protest.

"Does Hell intrude into Paradise, *mon ami?*" he said, with gentle raillery. "You have had twenty years of heaven on earth, you lucky devil, as I can witness. Must you still remember? If *she* can forget, why cannot you?"

The Sheik flung out his hand in quick remonstrance.

"If you had done what I did, would you have forgotten?" he cried, more bitterly than before. "But you, *bon Dieu!* you would never have stooped to such an infamy."

An odd look came over Saint Hubert's face, and he moved his head wearily on the pillow.

"Who knows?" he said slowly. "To win what you won I might even have done what you did. If the same temptation had come to me . . ."

His tired voice broke, and almost unconsciously his gaze went to the curtains that screened the inner room.

"Tout comprendre, c'est tout pardonner," he murmured. "She understood, and because she loved you she was able to forgive and forget. If, since then, you had ever failed her, or failed to keep her love, you might have just cause for bitterness.

"But you have made her happy all these years. Does that count for nothing, *mon cher?*"

"It is all that has made my life worth living," replied the Sheik huskily. "Without her love, and your friendship, God knows what I should have become."

And, ashamed of the sudden emotion that made his stern lips quiver, he rose abruptly and went to the table where were the papers that had been taken from the body of the man the Moor had killed.

Papers which were to prove of inestimable value to the Administration in dealing with the country, when, only a few months later, the stormcloud of the World War broke over France.

And, watching him as he stood scowling at the closely written documents he was turning over in his hands, Saint Hubert thanked God, as he had done many times during the last twenty years, for the strength that had enabled him to preserve that friendship.

Not even the love that consumed him had strained it, and the perfect comradeship had gone unbroken to the end.

The end! A little smile played over his lips. He could think of it calmly, he who had nothing to lose, nothing with which to reproach himself.

The woman he loved was happy, and if only he could keep off death until the girl returned, as return she would, he was convinced, he could die without a single regret.

But to die without knowing—*Dieu,* that would be hard!

He clenched his hand suddenly on the coverlet, as a stab of terrible pain shot through him, and for a few moments he lay with closed eyes, struggling against a deadly faintness, while the sweat of agony poured down his face.

It was a warning he could not ignore. If he was to learn what he wanted to learn, there must be no further delay. His weak call brought the Sheik back to his side in a couple of hasty strides.

"The Moor," he gasped. "I must see him now, if I am to see him at all. And I want to know for certain—before I go."

And looking down on the drawn grey face that had changed even in these last few minutes, the Sheik knew that he was speaking only the truth.

Yet still he hesitated.

"For God's sake, spare yourself this," he urged. "Let me see him alone...."

But Saint Hubert's feeble grasp tightened on his wrist.

"It can't make much difference, *mon cher,* and I want to see him myself—to hear the truth from his lips before I die," he said more firmly. "Send for him, Ahmed. It will make my going easier."

With a little nod, for words at the moment

were beyond him, the Sheik went to the open door and, clapping his hands softly, gave an order to the servant who was waiting within call.

The anxious friend had merged again into the Chief when he came back, and his face was hard and set, his black brows knitted in the formidable scowl as he drew his chair a little farther from the divan and sat down to wait in silence for the prisoner.

Conscious that but little strength was left to him, Saint Hubert also was silent as he lay, panting for breath, his eyes bright with feverish expectancy.

A soft-footed servant came noiselessly to relight the lamps that had been extinguished to cool the room.

After him, the scribe who was to take down the Moor's statement stole in with a deferential salaam, and squatted on the rug beside the Sheik, spreading his writing materials on his knee.

Then came Yusef and a couple of minor headsmen, who ranged themselves behind their Chief.

And, at last, after an interval which, short as it was, seemed to Saint Hubert like a century, the Moor came between his guards, his bandaged head held high, his blood-streaked face a mask of tigerish hate.

One glance he gave at the man he had shot, one furtive sweeping glance round the big, sumptuously furnished room, before he turned defiantly to the silent figure in the chair.

For a few moments the Sheik neither moved nor spoke.

Then, very slowly, he looked up.

"To all things and to all men there comes an end. And because through you the end came swiftly to certain of my servants, it is in my heart that your own end comes, but it may not be so swiftly.

"Some of the evil you have done, I know about. But I wish to learn more. If you want to die easily, tell me everything!"

The words came quietly, almost indifferently, the low-pitched voice carrying scarcely beyond the half-circle of armed men standing behind the prisoner.

But for all the smooth, even tone, there was something in the closing threat, something in the cold, steady stare fixed on him, that made the Moor's strange eyes flicker and his bound hands twitch suddenly.

"Since I die, I die silent," he snarled; "for what profit is there in talking?"

The Sheik shrugged, and a sinister look came into his eyes.

"What profit?" he echoed, with a terrible little smile. "Have you forgotten that there are many roads that lead to Paradise—or Hell? Listen, and when I have told you, choose then the way that you would go."

And in the same low, passionless voice as before, he spoke words that sent a quiver through the huge frame of the man who in his time had done so much and more to those unfortunates who had crossed his malign will, but who did not relish the prospect of himself experiencing what he had forced others to endure.

His savage pride revolting from the gripping terror that was turning his heart to water within him, desperately he fought to maintain the bold front he had assumed.

But his heavy breathing betrayed the fear he endeavoured to conceal, and great drops of moisture gathered thick on his forehead as he glared at the impassive face of his judge and then at the equally impassive faces of the men who surrounded him.

In them he saw his end, and the end of all his schemes and hopes, and he ground his teeth in a paroxysm of helpless fury.

It was Saint Hubert who broke the tense silence that had fallen on the room.

"Ahmed, for heaven's sake," he whispered protestingly, in English, "not that—not even to get the knowledge I want."

The Sheik looked back over his shoulder with a grim smile of amusement.

"Be easy. There will be no need to go to extreme lengths. He is sweating already. He will take the easier road.

"And, as for my methods of persuasion, they are no more than he promised the Boy when he had him in his power. Shall I offer him less than he offered my son?"

But the smile was gone when he turned again to the Moor.

"Must I wait all night—dog? *Choose!*"

Again the man's long, talon-like fingers plucked at the folds of his filthy burnous, and a foam gathered on the lips he was licking nervously.

For a moment longer he stood irresolute, struggling between pride and fear, glancing quickly from side to side as if still looking for some means of escape.

Then, with a twisted grin of rage:

"Since the mercy of my Lord is so great, what choice have I?" he sneered.

But as he spoke a change came over his manner, and the fine irony of his tone gave place to a note of ingratiating confidence, while words poured from him rapidly.

"What does my Lord desire to know?" he fawned. "The secrets of the *Roumi* who died yesterday? I don't know them. I was the *Roumi*'s guide, not the holder of his secrets. His secrets were in the papers he kept concealed beneath his robes.

"Last night I saw them taken from his body. Doubtless they are in my Lord's hands, to read—if you wish to. I know nothing about them, or what reasons brought him from his own land.

"But for me, O Master, must a man give reasons for seeking to avenge his honour, for searching for the daughter who is stolen from him?"

But the Sheik cut him short with a gesture of impatience.

"All that is known," he said sharply, "and we waste time. What I would hear deals not with the present, but with the past. . . ."

He paused for an instant, looking keenly at the dark, sweat-drenched face over which a mottled greyness was stealing.

"Yes, the past," he went on meaningly. "Last night you killed your master—but what of another master you killed—*O Ghabah from Morocco?*"

With a strangled cry the Moor reeled back against the man behind him.

"I didn't kill him," he gasped chokingly. "He died, but, by the head of the Prophet, I swear I didn't kill him."

"Yet, by the head of the Prophet, one swore he saw you kill him, and a dozen men besides, who sat unarmed round the dying embers of a camp-fire."

"He lied, for there were none left to see. . . ."

Too late he realised his mistake, and tried to check the impetuous words that were his own accusation.

For years he had thought the search abandoned, had thought himself safe.

But now he knew, and bitterly he cursed the folly that had brought him back to the land of his crime, that the search had never been abandoned, that always, unknown to him, the avenger of blood had stalked at his heels, tracking him relentlessly.

But who?

In a sudden flash of inspiration his bloodshot eyes rolled in the direction of Saint Hubert, and with a burst of mad laughter he sprang forward.

The Sheik leaped to intercept him.

But already the guards were round him, forcing him back, and from the knot of struggling men his voice rang out fiercely, exultantly:

"True, it is I who killed him. Not for gain, he was as poor as I.

"But one thing he had I craved, one thing that was his I longed to possess until the scorching fire of my desire drove me to slay that I might take that for which my soul burned.

"For three years these arms held her; for three years these eyes of mine saw all the wonder of her beauty. My slave she was, *mine, mine*—until I killed her for the coldness that turned my love to hate.

"Shall I tell you how she paid for that coldness before she died? Shall I tell you what I did before I killed..."

The Sheik's clenched hand crashed against the sneering, grinning mouth, beating it into silence.

"Enough that she died, you foul beast," he thundered. "What of her child?"

The Moor was rocking on his feet, his passion-swept features working hideously.

"The child I kept," he answered thickly, "that I might remember my hatred, that she too might remember that the Mother who bore her bore me no child—else I might have spared her."

Staring at him passionately, the Sheik put his last question.

"She is the girl—Yasmin?"

And the answer that meant so much came promptly.

"Yes, the girl who is called Yasmin." The torn lips curled maliciously. "Yasmin, the daughter of the proud French Sidi. Yasmin, whom it pleased my Lord's son to take as his plaything. Will he want her still, when the Alman has done with her?"

The mocking voice rose in a sudden shout, and with another wild burst of insane laughter the Moor fell back, writhing and twisting in the arms of the guards, blood streaming from his nose and mouth.

And long after he had been carried away, his ravings penetrated to the silent room where the Sheik was on his knees beside the divan.

He was striving with the tenderness of a woman to soothe the dying man, who lay with his face buried in the pillow, and shuddering with the horror that had broken him utterly.

"My God, my God, what she must have suffered!" He groaned. "If only I could have found her, only spared her some of that agony. Three years, Ahmed—think of it! God knows I searched. God knows I did my best. . . ."

With a quick murmur of protest the Sheik caught the hand that was tearing feebly at the coverlet.

"Raoul, Raoul," he cried imploringly, "for

my sake, for all our sakes, have some thought for yourself, I beg of you. . . . For her, thank God that it was only three years. It might have been longer.

"Forget it, *mon ami*. What good can come of remembering? You did all you could, no one could have done more. He must have been mad then; he's certainly mad now, and I can't shoot a madman, however much I want to."

Silence fell between them, and little by little the recurring fits of spasmodic shuddering grew less, till at last Saint Hubert lay still.

The cold grey light of the dawn had begun to creep into the room before he spoke again. Twisting painfully, he turned his head on the pillow, staring up at the weary face bent over him.

"The girl, Ahmed," he whispered faintly, "when the Boy brings her back . . ."

There was a world of entreaty in his questioning tone, and the Sheik's eyes dimmed with sudden tears.

"Mon ami, need you ask?" he said unsteadily. "The girl will be our care, Diana's and mine, if the Boy brings her back."

With a tired little smile Saint Hubert closed his eyes.

"He will—I know it," he murmured drowsily. "Let me see them when they come—and Caryll. But if I go before, give them my love, Ahmed, and for his own sake—tell Caryll, what he ought to know."

There was a little pause, then his hand went out gropingly and his voice came slower and more drowsily:

"Forty years, Ahmed, and nothing ever came —between us. It's a long time—a long time, *mon vieux* Ahmed. . . ."

* * *

In all his life Caryll never forgot that wild ride through the night. With the knowledge that only an hour or two of daylight remained, the start had been tempestuous.

He had ridden to hounds since boyhood, had joined in many a punishing chase across country, but never had he taken part in a hurricane race like this—a race for life or death that was fraught with grim and terrible purpose.

The exhilarating rush through the air, the thud of galloping hoofs behind him, the thought of what was impending, stirred in him an intense excitement he had never before experienced.

Only a few moments ago, for the first time, he had come up against murder and sudden death, had seen his best friend dying amidst a scene of ruthless slaughter and violence.

And swept completely out of himself, he had surrendered at last to inherited instincts and dormant impulses he had never even known to exist.

Convention had gone by the board, and, hostile and prejudiced no longer, tonight he was only his Father's son, one in mind and intent with this reckless band of stern and determined avengers.

And it seemed to him suddenly that all day long he had been moving towards this sense of sympathy and kinship, this acceptance of a relationship he had hitherto repudiated.

The day had been far different from what he had expected, and, more at rest within himself than he had been since leaving England, Caryll had even begun to be aware of a faintly dawning appreciation of his surroundings.

To see beauty he had never seen before in the golden expanse of desert stretched out round him, to feel and wonder at its curious peace and charm.

Before they reached the camp, sounds of wild tumult had warned them of some unusual happening, and the Sheik had spurred his mount into a headlong gallop.

Arriving, they had found the camp in an uproar; the big open space, usually so quiet, swarming with a densely packed mass of humanity, a confusion of sound and movement in which half-saddled horses, maddened by the general excitement, were breaking in all directions.

Screaming women and children were pushed this way and that as they clustered round the yelling crowd of gesticulating tribesmen mustering under the direction of Yusef and the Boy, whose ashen face was almost unrecognisable.

Events had followed with swiftness that left Caryll no time for thought.

He had seen the Sheik, his own face like death, stoop for a moment over the fainting messenger, from whom Gaston was trying to extract information.

He had taken and strapped about him mechanically the cartridge-belt and revolver thrust into his hands by a strangely pale but collected-looking Williams, and mounted the fresh horse which had appeared as if by magic beside him.

And almost before he had realised what was occurring or had taken in the full seriousness of the situation, he had found himself galloping towards the south, riding as he had never ridden before.

Not until El-Hassi was reached did he properly understand the peril through which his Mother had passed, or the fate that had overtaken Yasmin.

And the shock had shaken him beyond personal consideration, had forced him suddenly to a proper understanding of himself.

An understanding that had enabled him to recognise a claim that was greater than his own, that had made him able to put away hatred and envy, and rise above self.

He had turned down a page in his life's history when he had made the spontaneous offer which, uttered frankly and sincerely, had been so frankly and sincerely accepted.

And now, as he rode beside the brother he no longer hated, he was conscious that the strange disquietude of the last few days had passed as a nightmare passes.

He was able at last to think quietly, if not altogether dispassionately, of the brief madness that had aroused in him passions which now filled him with amazement and disgust.

It was not that he had ceased to love. He loved her still and knew that it might be long before the memory of his first love faded.

But the fierce fever of desire had burnt out as swiftly as it had flamed, and the love that was left was only the same pitiful tenderness he had felt for her before.

The rolling sand slopes had given place to almost level country, and, flat and featureless, the desert stretched ahead of them in unbroken monotony as they sped onwards, the wind whistling past their ears, the soft thud of galloping hoofs and the occasional sharp jingle of accoutrements the only sounds that broke the intense stillness.

For two hours they rode without slackening speed. Then, as little by little the light failed and dusk closed in round them, the pace moderated.

It grew gradually slower until at last the

tracker, who rode in front, flung up a hand, and, pulling in his horse, slid out of the saddle with a grunt.

A feeling of dismay came over Caryll as he glanced at the darkening sky, where only a few stars shone palely, and his heart sank at the thought of the hours that must elapse before the moon rose.

But almost before the thought formulated, the brief halt was over.

With a lighted lamp held close to the ground, the tracker took up the trail again on foot, pressing eagerly forward in a swift, tireless jog-trot he maintained without apparent effort.

On again until complete blackness enveloped them, until Caryll could only feel, rather than see, the shadowy outline of the figure riding beside him.

The men had broken rank somewhat, and once a horse blundered into his. And as he swung the kicking stallion clear, he heard a mumbled "Beg pardon, m'lord" come out of the darkness.

It made him suddenly wonder what Williams, who had refused to be left behind, was thinking, and whether his young enthusiasm had found satisfaction at last in the "real thing."

Time had slipped past without his knowledge, and in the soft light of the moon he had never noticed rising, he saw the Boy standing, talking to the tracker, and all about him the men dismounting and loosening the girths of their high-peaked saddles.

Slipping to the ground, he huddled into the coat that Williams was holding, and stamped to get the cramps out of his feet. Then he went to join his brother.

"What did the little Mother mean when she

said 'Isabeau de Chailles'? Who is Isabeau de Chailles?" the Boy asked him suddenly.

For a moment Caryll stared at him in blank astonishment. Didn't he know? Good God in heaven, didn't he know?

Then, quite suddenly, he remembered that Saint Hubert had told him that the Boy did not know, and he wondered bitterly why it had been left for him of all people to enlighten the man who had taken her so ruthlessly.

But it was better from every point of view that his brother should learn the truth, and learn it without further delay.

Smothering his own feelings, he told very briefly, with averted head, the story he had himself heard the night of the Boy's arrival.

And when he finished, his listener turned without a word, and went silently away.

It was not the track along which he had stumbled blindly that the Boy saw when at length he came to a halt, nor yet the glistening whiteness of the moonlit plain.

All he saw was a face—a delicate, oval face, with dark beseeching eyes that were misty and wet with tears, tears he had caused her to shed.

With a feeling of suffocation he tore at the heavy wrappings wound thickly about his throat. What difference did this story make?

Did they think he cared who she was! *Comtesse de Chailles*, or Yasmin the dancer—what did it signify to him? It was only the girl herself who mattered.

Only the girl herself he loved, whom in his heart he had never ceased to love, though in his rage he had denied it and sworn he hated her.

And with no thought for her pitiful weakness,

with no thought of his own strength, he had given full rein to all the innate savagery of his nature, and had exacted a terrible punishment for the treachery he imputed to her.

To satisfy his cruel and senseless vengeance he had stooped even to personal violence. In the madness of his rage he had tortured her—her, Yasmin, his tender, fragile flower.

Physically and mentally he had made her suffer, playing on her credulous fear and bruising with his merciless hands the lovely little body he would give his life to hold again, if only for a moment, in his arms.

She had loved him, he knew it now, loved him until the very end, loved him even when he had struck her.

Plainly, as on that last night, he could see the anguished tear-filled eyes, could hear the trembling, pleading voice, and a great sob burst from him.

"Allah, Allah, most merciful," he prayed, "that I may get to her in time—that I may be able to atone. . . ."

Riding again, it was easier to endure, and the rapid movement, the thunder of hoofs behind him, the rush of the soft night air against his face was oddly soothing, and brought him a feeling of new hope and courage.

Never before had he driven the black stallion as he was driving him now, never before had his sharp stirrups dripped blood as they were dripping now.

Lying almost flat on his horse's neck, the tracker long since outstripped and left behind, he rode with his burning, sand-caked eyes fixed only on the mingling hoof-prints that told of a race as speedy and precipitate as his own.

Mile after mile, and still with stirrup and voice he urged the gallant beast whose mighty limbs he could feel shivering and trembling between his knees.

And still Caryll and the tribesmen followed, strung out behind him, their bodies bent low in the saddle, their faces grey and ghastly in the pitiless light of the early dawn.

On, with only one thought. On, till his brain reeled and the heavy pounding of his heart drummed in his ears like the beating of a tom-tom.

On, till a pink flush crept over the eastern sky.

On, over ground that was again undulating.

On, past a low chain of rocky hills that had risen into view with startling suddenness and which masked the trail that, following the line of the hills, and skirting the base of the culminating cliff face, swung abruptly to the left.

At break-neck speed the Boy rounded the jutting rock spur in a wide, curving sweep, and then with a sharp sobbing breath flung himself back, hauling with all his weight at the stallion's mouth.

A village that had been, sand-swept and forlorn, with roofless huts and tumbled mud-brick walls, it stood chill and desolate in the cold half-light, seemingly tenantless and deserted.

But in the moment when he had emerged from behind the intervening rock, the Boy's straining eyes had caught a glimpse of a lurking, watching figure that had shrunk quickly back and disappeared amongst the ruins of crumbling houses, and he knew that the end of the long chase was here.

Weariness fell from him, and he was conscious only of a fierce, pleasurable excitement that dominated even the fear that tortured him.

He waited, fingering the heavy revolver he

had slipped from his waistcloth, until Caryll and the others swept into sight.

Then with a ringing shout he signalled them on, and, still a few paces ahead of them, bore down upon the village.

Yelling like the demons they were supposed to be, the tribesmen tore after him, fighting for the foremost places and bunching together as they neared the first little winding sand-heaped street.

At a headlong gallop, taking in his stride the drifts of rubble lying across his path, the big stallion shot up the narrow alleyway and out into a tiny open space that once had been the marketplace.

He was checked in a great slithering rush as the Boy wrenched him back, quivering, onto his haunches amidst a rattling hail of bullets.

The shots came from the dark entrance of a half-demolished roofed-in colonnade, but when the Boy's followers filled the square and an answering volley crashed out in return, the firing ceased abruptly.

And flinging himself out of the saddle, the Boy rushed for the dim passageway, with Caryll and the men racing after him.

Through a maze of gloomy, twisting turnings they sped, wondering at the absence of sound, wondering when would come the ambuscade that seemed inevitable.

Until as they pelted out into the daylight again, they realised the reason for the silence that had been so inexplicable.

Outnumbered, and with little heart left for an enterprise that had resulted very differently from their expectations, the rebels, after their first short show of resistance, had fled.

As the Boy and his followers poured through the broken archway into a wide street that gave on to the open desert, they saw the last of their opponents tumbling into the saddle to join their comrades who were already in full flight.

With a muttered word, the Boy waved on S'rir and a detachment of men in pursuit.

Reeling slightly, from fatigue, as he walked, he went with a numb feeling of dread through a little open courtyard.

On through a series of roofless rooms he went, stumbling unseeingly over piles of rubbish and debris, till he checked at last, shivering, at the entrance of a small apartment that stood whole and complete amidst the general ruin.

Instinct told him that here was what he had come to find, and for an instant he hung back, his clenched hands tightening until the nails bit deep into his palm.

Then very slowly he crossed the threshold and halted, his eyes searching the dimness of the squalid, ill-lit room.

A man was lying prostrate on the ground, his chest covered in blood, and in a far corner he saw her and thought she was dead!

Bearing all the marks of a desperate struggle, her unbound hair streaming over her bare shoulders, in her hand she held a dagger tipped crimson with the blood of the man who had tried to assault her.

Scarcely breathing, the Boy stood as if turned to stone, staring at the broken, pitiful little figure while one by one the boyish lines of his face were wiped out forever, and his features grew set and terrible.

"Yasmin!"

The hoarse cry of anguish broke from him like the cry of a soul in hell. Then with a scream she raised her head and sprung to her feet.

"*Lord!*"

Her slender arms outflung in passionate eagerness, she sped towards him.

With a groan that almost seemed to burst his heart, he swept her into his arms, crushing her to him with passionate strength.

"Yasmin, Yasmin."

Half-fainting, she lay against his chest as he rained kisses on her cheeks, her closed eyes, her lips.

At last the long wet lashes that were like a dusky silken fringe fluttered under his burning kisses, and slowly the tear-filled eyes that held only love and trust opened to meet his.

"Forgive me, my sweet, my little dove—forgive me—I love you—I have always loved you. Forgive me."

"What am I to . . . forgive?" she murmured humbly. "Am I not . . . yours to do . . . with as you want?"

Timidly one tiny hand stole up to clasp his neck.

"Lord, Lord, if you only knew how I love you . . . how I have longed for your love. You know now that I did not . . . betray you?"

His face went down on the tangle of dark hair lying against his breast.

"I know, I know," he answered brokenly. "May Allah forgive me—Yasmin, my love—Yasmin!"

Her hand touched his cheek, it was a caress, then she stiffened, for her fingers were wet.

"My Lord . . . I have . . . made you cry!"

"Because I am so happy that I have found you

—because you are mine now and forever, my love —my life—my wife."

She looked at him wonderingly.

"Y-your ... w-wife?" she stammered.

"My wife," he said firmly, "if you will—marry me after I have treated you so cruelly."

"You really ... mean that you will ... make me ... your wife?"

She spoke the words wonderingly, as if she could not believe what she heard to be true.

"If you will have me," he replied with a slight smile. But his arms tightened on her slender body possessively.

"I would want ... my son ... to bear his ... Father's name," she whispered.

"Yasmin!"

The Boy's exclamation was a cry of a triumph.

Then he was kissing her wildly, passionately, but combined with a tenderness she had never known before.

She kissed him back and a fire rose in him and his heart beat tumultuously against hers. Then lifting her in his arms he said softly:

"Let us go home, my beloved—home to my Mother and a new life where there in only love...."